WISTERIA WINDS

RACHEL HANNA

To my amazing, supportive husband. I couldn't do what I do without you always believing in my crazy ideas. I love you!

CHAPTER 1

DANIELLE STOOD BACK AND LOOKED AT MORTY. "ARE you sure you want to wear the wig?" she asked, laughing. Never in her life had she met someone who had fashion taste as flamboyant as Morty's, and she had lived in New York City for a while.

"Darling, without the wig, the entire ensemble is a total miss. Don't you read the fashion magazines? Wigs are en vogue these days."

The island was holding its first annual fashion show, and Morty was taking it very seriously. The prize was a fancy dinner and a show in Savannah, with Bennett supervising, of course. Danielle had spent all morning helping Morty prepare his "look", as he called it.

"What about these shoes?" Danielle asked, pulling a pair of reasonable black shoes from Morty's closet.

He stared at her. "Now, what man or woman has ever won a fashion show wearing clodhoppers like those?"

"Clodhoppers?"

Morty sighed and rolled his eyes. "Oh dear, are you even southern?"

She shrugged her shoulders. "Somewhat."

"First off, those shoes are reserved for weddings and funerals," he said, taking them from her and tossing them onto the floor of the closet. "And second, a man with my height issue needs something with a heel. Hand me those purple ones."

"But your suit is pink," she said, leaning into the closet to retrieve a pair of purple lace-up boots with thick platform heels. How a man in his late sixties could possibly wear such high heels was beyond her. She was almost forty and had given up those kinds of shoes years ago.

"Dear, you can never wear too many colors." Danielle had to laugh at that, considering her wardrobe was mainly neutral colors and black yoga pants. Of course, moving to an island that was very hot and humid most of the year meant she'd had to invest in lots of shorts and t-shirts.

"I don't think that's true, Morty. Your outfits may cause blindness. You might need a warning label on your forehead."

Morty giggled. "In all seriousness, do you think I

have a chance of winning this thing?" He stared into the full-length mirror in his bedroom and poked out one hip.

"Of course! Who has more style than you, Morty?"

"Well, Dorothy Monroe is participating, and she's got all those gowns she wore to award shows back in her heyday. The woman hasn't gained an ounce in decades, apparently."

"She is beautiful," Danielle said, looking off into space.

"Not helpful, dear."

"Sorry."

"And then there's Janice."

"The pink-haired square dancer?"

"Yes. Janice has a closet full of designer clothing from her daughter. I've seen Chanel in her closet, honey. Chanel!"

"Don't let those women scare you! You're Morty! You're unique and one of a kind. Who needs Chanel?"

He darted his eyes to the side and considered her words for a moment. "I do. I need Chanel." He sighed.

"Listen, I wish I had one tenth of your fashion sense."

He smiled, looking in the mirror at her standing behind him. "I wish that too. Those Jesus sandals you keep wearing have to go."

Danielle playfully slapped his shoulder. "Hey, I'm trying to be supportive!"

In reality, she shouldn't have been there, and Bennett would give her a lecture if he knew where she was. Danielle was the island nurse, and she was supposed to be impartial, even for a silly fashion show. She couldn't help that Morty had become like family to her. Many people said that, but didn't really mean it. She meant it. He was like the grandfather she never had, but better. Maybe he'd have been the cool uncle.

"I hope the weather isn't going to mess up the show," he said, trying on a new hat with a feather sticking out the side of it. Danielle had to wonder where he got this stuff. "Me too. They say the hurricane could hit this area head on, but that's at least a week away so it could change."

"Tell that Bennett not to reschedule my catwalk debut. My little heart couldn't take the devastation." He held his hand to the center of his chest and faked fainting, falling onto the bed behind him.

"Did you take drama in school?" It seemed like an obvious question with an even more obvious answer.

Morty laughed as he continued to lie on his back, looking up at the ceiling. "Lord no! I was very shy back in those days. I didn't quite know who I was yet. I mean, I was very outgoing in my mind, but I realized early on that it was too much for some people."

She sat down next to him. "So you made yourself smaller because you feared what other people thought of you?"

He sat up and put his finger on his chin. "I suppose you're right in that assertion. Hey, maybe that's why I'm so short!"

Danielle rolled her eyes. "I'm being serious!"

"I know, I know. I just don't like talking about all the serious stuff. Life's too… short!"

"Morty, you're a character," she said, laughing as she bumped her shoulder against his.

Bennett sat at his desk, a stack of papers calling his name out of the corner of his eye. Wisteria Island wasn't his only business, so he spent a lot of his day watching his stock portfolio and managing his other businesses. Thankfully, he had good people running most of them, and he wasn't nearly as hands-on with them as he was with the island.

Wisteria Island had his heart almost as much as Danielle did. Their relationship in the last few months had grown into something he didn't even know was possible. They ran the island together, caring for each resident like they were family. He adored watching her work with the residents. Her devotion to their healthcare was admirable, and he'd seen so many of them get better under her care.

However, caring for an island of older people who were only aging faster by the day had brought a new concern to light. Danielle was only one person, and as some residents required greater care, she was getting exhausted. They rarely went on actual dates, on or off the island. Danielle would get called at all hours of the night, and her days were filled with office visits and house calls.

Bennett hadn't taken the idea of aging into account when he decided to have one nurse on the island. His mind hadn't gone to the idea that some residents would need more care, more time, and more medical procedures. He had two options - bring in more help or force residents to move off the island right when they needed their support system most. It didn't seem fair or right to send them to awful nursing homes on the mainland just because they couldn't care for themselves at all anymore.

So, he'd decided to hire two new people. First would be a caregiver whose job would be to take care of the sickest residents. These were the people who would normally be in assisted living, memory care, or a nursing home. The caregiver would mainly help with medications, feeding, and transportation to and from medical appointments. Bennett had found a wonderful, experienced woman named Elise, and she was already working with a few residents who needed her.

Today he was interviewing a doctor for the island. After resisting it for so long, Bennett could now see that a full-time doctor who could do house calls, write prescriptions and diagnose more complex issues would not only help the island's residents, but would also free Danielle up a bit more. Maybe it was selfish, but he was hoping the doctor would give him more time with his own girlfriend.

"Doctor Emerson is here," Naomi said, popping her head through the doorway of Bennett's office.

"Oh, great. Send him in."

Doctor Zachary Emerson had come highly recommended from the recruiting agency Bennett hired. He didn't have the time or the inclination to sort through dozens of resumes, so he'd hired a medical recruiting firm to do it for him. One thing he'd learned as an entrepreneur was to hire people who were great at their jobs and not to try to do everything himself.

To his surprise, Doctor Emerson looked young, maybe even younger than him. He looked like he belonged on the front of a men's fitness magazine instead of in a white jacket with a stethoscope around his neck.

"Bennett Alexander?" he said, smiling as he walked through the door. He reached out his hand to shake Bennett's, his pearly white teeth almost blinding him. Bennett rarely felt insecure or inferior, but right now he felt like sucking in his stomach and making an appointment with his dentist for teeth whitening.

"Doctor Emerson, it's nice to finally meet you. I was very impressed with your resume. Have a seat."

"Please, call me Zach. This is a beautiful place you've got here. Eddie took me on a quick tour. This island was a very innovative idea."

"Thanks. And sorry you had to ride with Eddie. Do you need treatment for whiplash?"

Zach laughed. "It wasn't all that bad. I grew up on a farm in Tennessee, so we rode four wheelers every single day. A golf cart doesn't scare me."

Manly *and* smart. He must've been popular with the girls in high school.

"So, it says here you've worked with the geriatric community?"

"Yes. I've been exclusively working with them in hospitals and rehab centers for about six years now."

"You look too young for that to be true."

He chuckled. "I'm actually forty, but I've always had a baby face."

Forty? Bennett decided he had to get some wrinkle cream and fast.

"What kind of work did you do with them?"

"It has varied over the years, but I ran the geriatric unit at a rehab facility for a couple of years. We had patients who'd had hip and knee replacements, or who were recuperating from major falls. I also worked in the hospital in the geriatric unit. Then I started doing studies to figure out how we can increase longevity and the quality of living in our geriatric community."

Bennett realized this doctor was the only one he'd met with who had the experience to really help his residents. He could easily hit the ground running.

"What makes you want to work on our remote little island? I mean, I'm sure you have a social life?"

Zach chuckled. "Well, my last serious relationship was three years ago. I'm pretty focused on my work, and this place is perfect for the kind of research I'd like to do."

"When would you be able to start?"

"Immediately. My lease back in Nashville just ended, so I'm living in a hotel right now."

"I'd love to offer you the job then."

"Great! I can't wait to get started!"

Bennett stood up. "My assistant, Naomi, will help get you set up in one of the cottages. You'll be right next door to the island nurse, who also happens to be my girlfriend." For some reason, Bennett felt like he needed to say that, like some dog who peed on the neighborhood fire hydrant to mark his territory. Not that Danielle was anybody's territory. He figured that particular analogy was better kept to himself.

"Sounds good. I can't wait to meet with her to discuss our plans."

Danielle stood by the dock as she watched Jeremy drive the boat closer to the island. Bennett had asked her to wait for a new arrival. Getting a new resident on the island was always an exciting time for her because she loved to meet new people and see how she could help them. However, the island's residents weren't always so welcoming.

They seemed to be naturally suspicious of people, and she'd felt that when she first came to the island. It took a long time to build their trust, and even now, she was still working on that.

"Man, it's a windy day!" Jeremy said as he pulled the boat close to the dock and tied it off with a thick rope. The woman stood up carefully as the boat rocked back and forth a bit on the waves. This time of the year was particularly windy, with it being hurricane season. It would be Danielle's first hurricane season, and she was constantly watching the weather reports.

One worry she had about the island was the lack of transportation to the mainland. They had a couple of small boats, but there was nothing big enough to transport all one-hundred or so residents plus the employees.

"Welcome to Wisteria Island," Danielle called to the woman, smiling, as she stepped out of the boat. She was short, but on the rounder side, with curly brown hair and a paler complexion. Being a nurse, Danielle immediately wanted to check her iron and make sure she wasn't diabetic. There were signs she looked for in the residents, and she never wanted to miss an opportunity to treat someone before they had a major health event.

"Thank you. I'm Mamie Patterson. And you are?"

"Danielle Wright, the island's nurse. You'll be seeing a lot of me."

Mamie looked at her and furrowed her eyebrows. "Well, let's hope not."

"Oh, I didn't mean anything by that. I'm just very involved with the residents here. We believe in preventative medicine whenever possible."

"Honey, I've found that staying away from doctors and nurses is the very best kind of preventative medicine." She walked past Danielle and sat down in the golf cart while Jeremy loaded her bags.

Danielle was also tasked with taking her to her new home and helping her settle in. Eddie was apparently busy with some other pressing matter.

Danielle slid behind the steering wheel and looked over at Mamie, who was clutching her large handbag to her chest and staring straight ahead. Every new resident that came to the island arrived with their own baggage, both figuratively and literally. A student of the human psyche, Danielle wondered what Mamie was going to be like.

"Well, let's get you over to your new home," Danielle said as they started moving. She wasn't nearly the crazy driver that Eddie was. Instead, she liked to take a more leisurely pace as she showed new residents all that the island offered. "Your cottage is over on Seashore Road. It's one of the most beautiful parts of our wonderful island."

"That's nice. I lived in a landlocked area for most of my life, so I'm quite looking forward to a pretty view."

"You'll also be close to the cafeteria, which is actually more of a diner. And my office isn't far from there."

"Good to know."

Danielle turned down one road and continued pointing out important places. "This is where you can get mail, and over here is the activity center." Mamie turned her head and looked, taking in her new environment. "So, what brings you to Wisteria Island?"

She looked at Danielle. "Well, I'm getting old, and I had the money to live here. What else would bring me here, dear?"

"Of course," Danielle said, feeling like a scolded child. "And here we are. Your house is that adorable little yellow one there."

Mamie groaned. "I hate yellow. Such an ugly color. Nobody wears it well."

"Oh, I don't know. I think yellow is a sunny color," Danielle said, smiling as she pulled up in front of the cottage.

It really was a cute place. It was one of the newer cottages, with a front porch that extended the entire length of the house. With bright white spindles and two rocking chairs on either side of the front door, Danielle kind of wished she lived there.

Her own cottage had undergone all kinds of repairs in recent months, and she was glad for that. Darryl had done a lot of work being the only handyman on the island. But there was still something to be said for a beautiful new cottage.

"I suppose it will work. I'm not going to be standing outside looking at it all that often. I'm not much for the outdoors."

"Maybe living on the beach will change that. We

have many activities, including beach parties and the walking club."

"I might just get involved in that. I like to be in the thick of things."

Danielle took one of her bags and walked toward the front door, pulling her keys out of her pocket. As they entered, Mamie started looking around.

"What do you think?"

"It's nice. Not quite as big as my condo in Atlanta, but it will do."

"I'll just go put these bags in your bedroom." Danielle turned to the left and walked down a short hallway. The cottages only had two bedrooms, so she chose the one with the adjoining bathroom and set Mamie's bags on her bed.

"So, how long did you live in Atlanta?" Danielle asked, as Mamie followed behind her.

"Fifteen years. Until my husband died five years ago, I never expected to leave."

"I'm sorry for your loss."

Mamie sighed and then sat down on the edge of the bed, Danielle following suit. "Thank you. He was a wonderful man. We'd known each other since grade school. It's not easy to find and keep a love like that."

Danielle agreed. Her relationship with Bennett was still so new that she was learning things about him all the time. Quirks, personality traits, family history. Mostly, she was impressed, although he had his own tendencies that sometimes annoyed her.

For one thing, he chewed loudly. She'd never heard anybody chew so loud. She was convinced he had a hole somewhere in his head because the sound of him crunching on potato chips would reverberate through any room, even though his mouth was closed.

But then there was his kindness, his thoughtfulness, his sense of humor. The good most definitely outweighed the bad. He was nothing like her ex fiancé Richard. Bennett was a good man with a good heart. Everybody knew that.

"Everyone should be so lucky to have one great love of a lifetime," Danielle said.

"I suppose so. I'm going to put my favorite framed picture of him right there by my bedside."

"If you don't mind me asking, do you have any children?"

"I do. A son and a daughter. My son, Charlie, is currently living in the Philippines. He teaches English at a university there. My daughter and I don't have a great relationship. I suppose a lot of mothers and daughters go through something like that."

"I'm sorry to hear that. Does she know you've moved here?"

"No. We haven't spoken in the last two years. I miss her a lot."

Danielle wondered what broke their relationship apart, but she wasn't about to ask. She had only just met Mamie, and she was trying to build a good rapport with her. The last thing she wanted to do was overstep her boundaries.

"Thank you for showing me to my cottage, but if you don't mind, I think I might want to take a little nap now."

Danielle nodded and stood up. "Of course. Just so you know, dinner is at six o'clock tonight. I think we're having tacos, which are always a favorite around here."

"Wonderful. I'll make sure to be there so I can meet some of my new neighbors. I love to ask questions and find out what makes people tick."

"Well then, we have something in common. I hope to see you at dinner, Mamie." Danielle walked out of the room and then out the front door before climbing into the golf cart. She was looking forward to getting to know more about Mamie, but right now she didn't have a good grasp on who the woman was. She'd have plenty of time to figure that out, as she cared for her in the years to come.

CHAPTER 2

"FRANK, HAVE YOU BEEN HAVING ANY PAIN AROUND your scar?" Danielle asked as she palpated Frank's upper right quadrant. It hadn't been that long ago since he had come to her door in the middle of the night with pain that resulted in him having his gallbladder removed. In his eighties, Frank was definitely someone she kept a close eye on.

"No pain. I do get a lot more gas these days."

"That's to be expected. Your gallbladder provided an important part of your digestive system. Your liver must work overtime now, and you may not be able to digest some foods as easily as you once did. There's actually a supplement I can give you to help whenever you're going to eat something with fat in it."

"That would be great. Thanks, Dani." Most of the

residents called her Dani, although she had convinced Bennett to call her Danielle. She just preferred her longer name, but she didn't mind that the residents called her by her nickname.

"I think we're all finished here. Here are those supplements. I'll give you just a few to try. Take one as soon as you eat a bite of food that has fat in it."

"Like tonight at taco night?"

Danielle laughed. "Exactly." She waved as Frank walked out the front door and was happy to have a few minutes of alone time in the clinic. She'd been so busy over the last couple of weeks. September always brought viruses and flu, and this September was no exception. Even though people rarely went off the island, it only took one person going into town to bring it back to the entire island. They had to be very careful about that.

"Danielle?" She heard Bennett calling from the waiting room. There was nothing better than a surprise visit from her boyfriend in the middle of the day.

She opened the door to find Bennett standing in the waiting room with another man she'd never seen before. He looked to be around her age, maybe a bit younger, and he was wearing a white doctor's coat.

"Oh. Sorry, I didn't know you were bringing company."

The man stepped forward and reached out his

hand. "Dr. Zachary Emerson. It's nice to meet you. Bennett has told me a lot about you."

She stood there looking like a deer in the headlights. "He has? I apologize, but I don't think he's mentioned your name to me before."

Bennett smiled. "Sorry. It was kind of a surprise for you."

"I don't understand. You got me another man as a surprise?"

"I might have phrased that the wrong way," Bennett said, laughing. "What I meant was that I wanted to surprise you by hiring a new full-time doctor for the island. I wanted to take some of the stress off of you."

Danielle didn't know what to say. He'd hired a doctor without telling her? Without consulting her at all? Why didn't he just hire an additional nurse? So many questions, but she didn't want to be rude in front of Dr. Emerson.

"Oh. I see. Very nice to meet you, Dr. Emerson."

"Please, call me Zach."

"Great. Nice to meet you, Zack. Bennett, can we talk in private for a moment?"

"That's never a good thing," Zach said under his breath. He walked over and sat down in one of the chairs, looking down at his phone, obviously uncomfortable.

Without a word, Bennett followed Danielle to the

back. She took him into one of the examination rooms and closed the door. "You hired a doctor without even asking me?"

"Danielle, you're always exhausted. We barely have any time to spend with each other. I thought this was a good thing."

"A good thing would've been to ask me if I wanted that help. I have a system now. These people trust me, or at least most of them. And now you're throwing a brand new person into the mix?"

"So you don't want me to hire him?"

"So you haven't already hired him?"

Bennett looked down at the floor for a moment. "He signed his contract a bit ago."

Exasperated, she threw up her hands and leaned against the table. "Bennett, how do you know I'll even get along with this guy? If you wanted to help me, why didn't you just hire another nurse?" She hated to sound sexist, but her experience in hospitals had shown her that male doctors had superiority complexes that made their heads hard to fit into the rooms.

"I figured having a doctor on the island would be great for the residents and would certainly attract more people to want to live here. He can do things you can't do, like order certain tests or prescribe medications. I'm sorry. I really wasn't trying to step on your toes, and if you want me to send him off the island, I'll do it."

"You'll vote him off the island?" she joked, referring to their favorite reality TV show.

"I'll vote him off in a heartbeat," he said, winking at her.

She stood there for a moment, her arms crossed. She wanted to be angry, but he had a point. Having a doctor on the island would save her so much time having to take patients back-and-forth to the mainland. Plus, they could get a lot more done between the two of them. She was wearing herself out, trying to care for almost one hundred people alone.

"Fine, I forgive you. But the next time you could at least give me the courtesy of talking to me first. This was a pretty big decision to make without asking the island nurse. I'm not even talking about being your girlfriend."

He smiled and slid his hands around her waist. "I love when you call yourself my girlfriend."

She laughed. "What else am I supposed to call myself?"

"I'd better get out there to finish my tour with Zach."

"You're not giving him my office, are you?"

"Of course not, silly. We have that extra office that we're using for storage. I'm going to have Darryl clean that out for me."

Together, they walked back out into the waiting room where Zach was sitting, watching people walk down the sidewalk. "Oh, are we ready to continue the tour?"

"Absolutely. I know Danielle has some patients this afternoon, so we will get out of her hair. She needs to have a break. She's been working awfully hard."

Danielle rolled her eyes. "He makes it sound a lot tougher than it really is."

"Do you think the residents here will accept me?"

She shrugged her shoulders and laughed. "The only thing I can tell you about the people here is that they are unpredictable. Some of them will accept you, but some of them will give you a run for your money and put you through your paces."

"I can't wait to hear the backstory on that. I'll see you tomorrow?"

"Oh, are you not coming to dinner tonight?"

Zach looked at Bennett. "What's this about dinner?"

"We all eat dinner together every night in the cafeteria. It's just a way for the residents to get to know you and feel like they have direct access. I'll show you where that is again, just so you know."

He smiled. "It's gonna take me a little bit to get acclimated to this place, but I really like it so far."

They turned and walked out, with Bennett waving to Danielle one more time. She smiled, but she had to admit that she wasn't sure how this was going to work. She had developed her own methods and plans for how she worked with the residents, and she wasn't so sure about having another person's opinion inserted into her daily life. Plus, she was still a little irritated that Bennett hadn't talked to her first.

She knew he was doing it for a good reason. He wanted her to have more free time to spend with him, and he also didn't want to see her so stressed out. But having to share duties and agree with another medical professional all the time might've been more than she wanted to deal with.

Danielle walked into the cafeteria with Zach beside her. Bennett had asked her to show him around and make sure he interacted with the residents because he had an important call that had come in back at the office. Danielle was pretty sure Bennett was trying to push her to spend time with Zach, so she wouldn't be mad at him for hiring a doctor without even talking to her.

"So this is the cafeteria, huh? Looks more like a very large diner."

She laughed. "Yeah, it's not your typical cafeteria for sure."

"How does this work, exactly?"

"Well, you go down that line over there to choose your sides. The entrée each night is the same for everyone. Then there is the dessert cart, the coffee bar and the soda fountain, as most of the residents call it. You choose a table and chat with the residents. Easy peasy!"

"Easy peasy? Is that official medical terminology?"

"You learn to abandon the medical terminology on Wisteria Island. If you even start mentioning white blood cell counts or magnetic resonance imaging, you'll get some very bored stares. Keep things simple and light."

"And what if something is serious? Not every medical condition can be simple and light."

She turned and looked at him. "Bennett said you've worked with the geriatric community before. Was that a lie?"

"It wasn't a lie. It was just more of a clinical setting."

She looked back over at the ever-growing line as her stomach growled. "Well, just think of Wisteria Island as the least clinical place on earth. The people here want to be happy and carefree, and we give them that as much as possible. Now, come on. I'm starving. I hope you like tacos."

He followed behind her as they got in line. She took two beef tacos along with the fixings, such as Spanish rice, shredded cheese, lettuce and tomatoes. When they got to the end, Danielle walked to an empty table and set her tray down.

"Can I get you something to drink?" Zach asked after he put down his tray.

"Sweet tea. Thanks." Just as Danielle was about to dig into her first taco, Gladys sat down next to her. She almost always had dinner with Gladys, so it wasn't a big shock.

"Hey, Dani!"

"Hey there, Gladys. How was your day?"

"Boring. My IBS is flaring up, and I couldn't get ten feet away from the bathroom all day."

Danielle stared down at her ground beef filled taco and set it back on her plate. Gladys really knew how to kill her appetite. "You didn't tell me you were having issues."

"Well, I didn't want to bother you with it. I know you've got bigger fish to fry."

"I have medications that can help you with that. Come see me tomorrow, okay?"

"Okay." Zach walked back over and set her glass of tea in front of her, placing a glass of water with lemon

in front of his plate before sitting down. Gladys stared
at him like she was seeing a two-headed alien. "Good
Lord, where did this hunk of burning love come from?"

Danielle choked on her tea and almost spit it
across the table. She quickly grabbed a napkin to
wipe her mouth. "Gladys!" She looked at Zach, biting
her lip. "Sorry about that."

He smiled at Gladys. "I will never be offended by
someone calling me a hunk. Trust me. I'm Dr.
Zachary Emerson." He reached across the table and
shook her hand. Danielle swore there were literal
stars in Gladys' eyes.

"Nice to meet you," she said, resting her chin in
her hand and batting her eyelashes.

"There's nothing wrong with her libido, as you
can see," Danielle whispered to Zach. He stifled a
laugh.

"So, are you here for a visit, Dr. Zach?"

"Dr. *Emerson* was hired to work on the island full
time," Danielle said, telling Gladys the proper name
to call the doctor.

Gladys beamed. "You know, Dr. Emerson, I have
this pain in my lower back I might need to see you
about…"

"Gladys, stop flirting with him!" Danielle said,
tapping her on the arm. Gladys shrugged her
shoulders.

"You can't blame a lady for trying. Do you know

how long it's been since I had a boyfriend? Literally, there were dinosaurs."

Zach chuckled. "I consider it an honor that Gladys is flirting with me."

She turned a shade of red Danielle hadn't seen before. "Oh darn! I forgot to get some peach cobbler. I'll be right back."

Gladys wandered away, stopping at other tables as she made her way to the dessert bar. If history told her anything, Danielle knew Gladys wouldn't come back to the table until her food was almost cold. She had become quite the social butterfly.

"She's a hoot!" Zach said, taking a bite of one of his tacos.

"Yes, she is. When I started working here, they thought she had dementia or even Alzheimer's. I was able to work with her and find out that it was an adverse reaction between medications she was taking. She's doing so much better now."

"That's amazing, Danielle. So many medical professionals don't take the time to really dig deep and find the root cause of a patient's issue. I mean, just because she's older doesn't mean she doesn't deserve to get quality medical care."

She smiled. "Thank you. It really means a lot to hear someone else within the medical community say that. A lot of my friends think I took a big step down coming to work at a place like this. But just because they are older people doesn't mean they don't want to live full, healthy lives. Some of them are happier than my younger friends."

"You know, I worked at this long-term rehab center a few years ago. I was appalled at the care these patients were getting. I filed a formal complaint, and they ended up firing me for insubordination."

That made Danielle livid. "Seriously? Because you complained about the treatment of the patients?"

"Yes. I was astonished. I think our society is really disrespectful to our elderly. We treat them like trash sometimes. So many kids don't even come to visit their parents in these nursing homes I've visited."

She nodded her head, taking a sip of her tea. "It's a common problem. Once a quarter we have a family visit here on the island. I would say more than half the residents don't get any visitors at all. It's like their families just put them here because they were problematic. Granted, our residents tend to skew toward the eccentric side, but I've seen so many of them just be abandoned."

"Good evening, darlings!" Morty said, walking up to the table and twirling around. He loved to twirl. It was definitely his signature move. Tonight's ensemble included a pair of faded black jeans, cowboy boots, and a red pearl snap button-up shirt that looked like something out of a cowboy movie. Well, if a cowboy movie was also set in a seventies disco club.

"Hey, Morty. Have you met Dr. Zach Emerson?"

Morty looked at him carefully. "No, I don't believe I've had the pleasure. Are you an actual doctor or just a model playing a doctor?"

Danielle laughed. "You'll have to excuse Morty. He's our resident comedian."

"Nice to meet you, Morty. I've taken a job here on the island."

Morty's eyes widened. "Really? I'll have to make an appointment about some issues I've been having."

Danielle stared at him. "Oh really? So you're not going to see me anymore?"

"Well, I thought I'd give the good doctor a chance to see if he can figure out some of my other issues."

"What other issues? I've worked with you on everything from gout to high blood pressure."

He lightly slapped her on the shoulder. "Don't tell him my secrets! You're making me sound like an old man."

"Well, we wouldn't want to do that," Danielle said, rolling her eyes. She was surprised at how Gladys and Morty had been so accepting of Dr. Emerson since they had given her such a hard time when she started. She could only assume it was because Dr. Emerson was more than handsome. He had those catalog model good looks. Actually, he looked more like a leading man in a romance movie.

Still, she didn't consider herself to be homely or ugly. She was pretty, but not in the supermodel sort of way.

"Well, welcome to the island. I need to run over there and show my friends this new shirt I got. Ordered it right off the Internet. Would an old man do that, Dani?"

She laughed. "It's a lovely shirt, Morty."

He laughed and waved before trotting away toward a table full of his friends. Most of the people on the island loved Morty, which was a good thing, since his own family seemed to be completely absent from his life. It made Danielle sad every time she thought about it because Morty was an amazing human being. Whatever the history was with his family, she couldn't believe anybody would ever abandon him.

"This place is crazy," Zach said, smiling. "I think I'm really going to enjoy it here. Everybody is so full of life."

"There are a few of them that can be quite difficult. Dorothy Monroe is one to remember. She was a famous actress in her day, and she came in here with a lot of ego that did not go over well with the other residents."

"Oh, really?"

"She's settled down a lot now. I realized she was suffering with some depression, so medication has helped her a lot. I even saw her at bingo the other night."

"You're really involved around here, aren't you?"

"You have to be. Gaining the trust of these people was really hard for me, but then again, I don't look like a movie star."

He rolled his eyes. "I don't look like a movie star. I look like my dad."

Danielle had to wonder what his dad looked like. "Well, either way, you'll probably run across at least a few people that will give you some trouble. Oh, and I do have one really important piece of advice."

"What's that?"

"Stay away from the nude beach."

Zack's eyes widened. "The what?"

CHAPTER 3

Mamie sat at her table alone, waiting for anybody to show up. She had always hated being the new person. Growing up in a military family, she moved at least once a year, constantly changing schools. She hated it at the time, but as an adult, she realized it had given her some special skills.

For one thing, she could slide into pretty much any social situation and fit in. She had no fear of asking people questions and getting to know them because she'd had to do it so much as a kid.

Second, it made her like a chameleon. She could fit herself into all kinds of situations without appearing to be out of place. It made people trust her, and she didn't really trust people. It was kind of an odd combination.

"Are you new here?" A woman stood in front of

her, holding a tray with two tacos and a glass of water. Mamie could already tell she was probably a pretty boring person.

"Yes, I am. Care to sit down?"

"I guess so," the woman said, setting her tray down and sliding into the seat. She was tall, thin and wore very expensive clothes. Mamie was sure that suit she was wearing was Chanel, although she couldn't imagine why anyone would come to taco night wearing such a thing.

"I'm Mamie Patterson. And you are?"

The woman's lips looked like they had just sucked on a very sour lemon, and one eyebrow was raised in the air. Her hair, unmovable, was a mixture of black and gray. "Dorothy."

Mamie held out her hand, but Dorothy ignored it, looking down at her taco and cutting it up with a fork. A fork? Who did that? Mamie was always full of questions. Her mother said she asked so many that she was going to hit her quota before she ever got to heaven to ask God any pertinent ones.

"Nice to meet you, Dorothy. How long have you been here?"

"A few months."

"Do you like it?"

Dorothy glared at her. "Do I enjoy being an old woman who is forced to live out on an island because her own family doesn't want her? Not particularly. But am I getting more used to it and surviving? I guess."

Yikes. Mamie didn't know what to think about this woman. She certainly didn't seem like she should be on the welcoming committee or anything.

"Well, I have two kids that are busy with their lives. One is in another country and the other one doesn't speak to me, so I get what you mean."

"I don't have any kids."

Mamie said nothing else and chose instead to look down at her tacos. She filled them with just about every topping, and now she regretted that decision since she had to figure out a way to eat them that wouldn't squirt the red sauce all over her brand new pink T-shirt.

"Mind if I ask what you did in your younger years?" Dorothy stared at her.

"Why does it matter?"

"I know this is way off base, but you look so much like this actress I used to love watching in movies when I was younger. Her name was Dorothy Monroe, so I thought maybe there was a chance…"

Dorothy's eyes lit up just a little bit. Mamie could tell she was making progress.

"That's me. I'm sure this isn't exactly the place you thought I might end up."

She couldn't believe she was sitting across from *the* Dorothy Monroe. Mamie wasn't lying when she said that she had been a huge fan of hers back in her youth. Dorothy was a hot commodity for a long time. Then she sort of disappeared from films.

"I can't believe I'm getting to have dinner with Dorothy Monroe. I don't know how you ended up living here on Wisteria Island, but I'm glad to get to meet you. I loved that one movie you did where you became a famous singer and had a show in Vegas. What was that one called?"

"The Last Song in Vegas?"

"That's right! Did you do your own singing?"

"I actually did. I had a very good voice back in my younger years. Not so much these days."

"A lot of things change as we get older, I suppose," Mamie said. One thing she was great about was forming connections with people. She found that gaining people's trust made them open up, and she could get a lot more information from them.

"They do. When you're young, you think every-thing will always go your way. You think your family will always love you and take care of you. In the end, people just let you down. I guess it's just the way of the world."

"So, you mentioned you don't have children? Do you have any extended family?"

"I do have a few nieces. But nobody comes to see me. They only cared about me for my money, apparently."

Sometimes, Mamie felt bad for what she was so good at. In her decades as a tabloid reporter, she had cracked some of the biggest stories in Hollywood. These days, she just did it for fun. She liked to find out about people's lives, and she loved asking questions.

But if she was honest with herself, she missed the thrill of the chase. She missed breaking the story. Her career was long before the Internet, but she could only imagine how incredibly successful she would've been posting her stories online.

Honestly, she didn't really understand how the Internet worked. She wasn't sure how people made money, and she was way too old to try to figure it out. But it would not stop her from finding out as much gossip as possible on Wisteria Island.

"I'm sorry to hear that. This younger generation is just something else."

"I guess you could say that."

"So, tell me, what are the best activities to get involved with here on the island?"

Dorothy shrugged her shoulders. "I'm not exactly the most social person, as you can probably imagine. But I have done bingo and gotten involved in a book club. I'm starting to at least make some acquaintances, but I wouldn't call them friends yet."

"I love bingo, and I wouldn't mind joining a book club. Maybe you can give me more information?"

"Of course. I'll be glad to after we eat."

As Mamie sat there, smiling and eating her tacos, she formulated a plan. Wisteria Island needed to be more exciting, and she was definitely the one to make sure that happened.

Danielle sat on her back porch overlooking the ocean, taking in long deep breaths of the sea air. Her favorite time of day was after dinner when she could sit outside and just barely see the whitecaps racing toward her under the light of the moon. The sound of the waves coming in and out was the most soothing thing in the world to her.

Most evenings, she could be found sitting in her rocking chair on the back deck, drinking a cup of decaf coffee. She had learned over the years not to have caffeine after about five o'clock or else she would be up all night long. Of course, she put so much sugar in her coffee that sometimes that alone kept her up.

"Hey there," Bennett said, walking around the corner. Their relationship had become so easy and predictable, and neither of those were bad things as far as she was concerned. He knew exactly where she'd be at any given time of day. Of course, on such a small island, it wasn't hard to find people. It wasn't exactly a place you could go hide out.

"Hey. I missed you at dinner," she said, looking up at him. He leaned over and gave her a quick kiss before sitting down in the chair next to her. She could tell he was upset about something, especially when he leaned back and sighed, putting his hands over his eyes. "What's wrong?"

"I have to leave the island for a while."

"What? Why?"

"My great aunt is very sick. I know I don't really have a lot to do with my family, but she was the only one besides my mother that I ever really had a relationship with. I keep in contact with her mostly through video chat and the occasional email. Her daughter contacted me right before dinner and told me she wasn't expected to make it another week."

"Oh, Bennett, I'm so sorry. I remember you mentioning her a couple of times. So you're going to visit her?"

"Yeah. She lives in Louisiana, so I'm going to start driving tomorrow morning. I'd like to spend some time with her before she passes away."

"So you're going to rent a car?"

"Yes. I would fly, but getting a private plane so quickly isn't easy, and I like to have my own transportation, anyway. It'll take me a while to get there, but I can use that time to clear my head a bit. She's older, so this shouldn't be unexpected, but I still feel terrible that I haven't seen her much in the last three years."

"You've been kind of busy with this island. Why didn't she come to live here?"

He laughed. "She told me in no uncertain terms that she didn't want to come live on my 'old folks island'. Besides, she's very close to her daughter and lives in her guest house."

"Well, I will miss you. I wish I could go."

"I do too. But at least you have Zach here to help you keep things running. You can stand in my place pretty well at this point."

"I don't know about that. Some of these residents still give me a hard time, you know."

He laughed. "You don't give yourself enough credit. Everybody here loves you, and they trust you. That's exactly what I was hoping for when I hired you."

"Did you eat dinner?"

"I had a pack of saltines and a can of ginger ale that I found in the vending machine."

Danielle rolled her eyes. "That's not dinner. Why don't I cook something for you? Maybe some spaghetti?"

He smiled. "That would be fantastic."

∾

Danielle spent the next morning seeing Bennett off. It would not be the same without him on the island. Sometimes she worried she was getting too attached. The last thing she wanted was to have another relationship fall apart and find herself devastated in the process.

Of course, when she broke up with Richard, it really wasn't all that devastating except for the fact that she was thoroughly embarrassed by his antics. This time, she was really in love. More in love than she could ever imagine. Breaking up with Bennett might destroy her, even though the feminist inside of her didn't want to admit that.

"Good morning." Zach came walking through the door, startling her. She was used to having the first hour to herself before patients started showing up. It was going to take some time to get accustomed to having someone working in the same office as her.

"Good morning. Are you ready to get started today?"

"I am at your command."

She chuckled. "You're the doctor. I'm just a lowly nurse."

He rolled his eyes. "I could feel the sarcasm from across the room. Besides, I happen to think nurses are the unsung heroes of the medical system. Doctors get way too much credit." She liked him already.

"Well, we have a few appointments this morning. I thought maybe you could sit in on those, kind of get an idea of how I work?"

"That sounds great. I'd like to get to know as many of the residents as possible. What kinds of things do you do outside of the office?"

"I do some house calls. I love to do health fairs where I get everybody together and take blood pressure, blood sugar, that sort of thing. I also do some health lectures from time to time. I've taught them about proper nutrition, making green smoothies and juices, a little bit of yoga."

"Wow. So you truly are a one stop shop."

She smiled. "I really love working here. I didn't think I would, and I almost left. In fact, there were eight nurses before me in the previous three years and all of them left."

He stared at her, his eyes wide. "Seriously? Eight nurses?"

Danielle started laughing. "Trust me, when I found that out, I almost swam back to shore."

"I imagine so. Why did so many leave?"

"Well, part of it was that these residents can be a bit difficult. They aren't your typical retirees. Many of them have been abandoned by their own families, shuffled off to this island because they are eccentric or quirky."

"And the other part of it?"

"I think some of it was the cottage. When I got here, the thing looked like it was going to fall to the ground. But that has been remedied."

"My cottage is actually pretty nice."

"I'm sure it is, *Doctor,*" she said, emphasizing the doctor part. "Anyway, before I came here, I was an ICU nurse at one of the top hospitals in the country. Then some things fell apart, and I ran here like a kid runs away from home. At first I thought I had made a big mistake."

"Why did you give up the ICU?"

She continued going through one box of supplies, partially counting out how many she had and what she needed to replenish. "It's a long story, and I have to know you a lot better before I tell it to you."

He smiled. "Oh, I understand. I have some of those stories myself."

"Anybody in here?" a man called from the waiting room. Just by the sound of his voice, Danielle knew it was Ted.

"Mr. Donovan?" Danielle said, walking back into the waiting room.

"I told you to call me Ted. "

"Actually, you first told me to call you Theodore until we were friends. What are you doing here? I don't have you on my calendar until next week."

"Well, my hip is kind of hurting me. I think it

might be because me and the wife got a little too amorous the other night..."

She held up her hand just as Zach appeared behind her. "You really don't have to give me any more information."

"Who is this guy?"

Danielle turned around and quietly whispered to Zach. "Here's your trial by fire."

"Hi, Mr. Donovan. I'm Dr. Zach Emerson. I've just taken a position on the island."

"Wait just a cotton pickin' minute. You're not leaving us already, are you, Danielle?"

She watched as the old man furrowed his eyebrows together, the wrinkles so deep between his eyes that she could've easily lost a quarter in there. "No, sir. Bennett hired Dr. Emerson just to have an extra set of hands here on the island. Plus, he can order medication and different testing that I can't without taking you to the mainland."

"I see. Well, Danielle takes care of me. I don't want another doctor."

"I totally understand, sir. When you get comfortable with someone, you don't want things to change. I'm just here to be extra help, but I won't be stepping on Danielle's toes. She's done wonderful things here."

Danielle had a warm, fuzzy feeling in her stomach. She was so happy to hear that Zach would not be trying to change everything. He didn't seem to have that common doctor ego that she'd run across so many times in the hospital system. He actually seemed like a pretty nice, down-to-earth guy.

In fact, he would've been the type of guy she would've been interested in dating before she came to Wisteria Island and met Bennett. Unfortunately, she hadn't run across a lot of doctors who were like him. She ran across plenty who were like Richard.

"Why don't you come on back, Ted? We can take a look at that hip."

Zach followed her back to the room, being careful to stay in the background and listen to her conversation with Ted. She was impressed with how he didn't try to jump in and give his two cents' worth, obviously sensing that Ted was someone who required a lighter touch.

"Right there. Is there a bruise?" he asked, craning his neck.

"No, there's not. It seems like maybe you just strained a muscle here. I would take some anti-inflammatories, but be sure you have food in your stomach. If it's hurting longer than another forty-eight hours, come back and talk to me. You might also even want to do an Epsom salt bath."

Danielle had found that when she tried the easiest things first, her patients had better outcomes. So often, doctors went straight to heavy prescription medication, causing additional symptoms. And then they ended up in a situation where they had tons of pill bottles sitting on the kitchen counter, each of them interacting with each other.

"All right then. Just glad to know I didn't break it or anything."

She smiled as he stood up and put his hat back on his head. "No, no breaks. But you and the Mrs. might want to settle down a bit. Your bones are a little more brittle than they used to be."

Ted grumbled and shook his head, walking out the front door. When people refer to an old codger, Ted's picture probably came up in the dictionary next to it.

"Wow. He was something else."

"Yes. The first time he came to see me, it was about erectile dysfunction. That was quite an interesting visit."

Danielle turned around and went into the back, pulling up the day's schedule on her tablet. Her first patient shouldn't arrive for at least another half an hour, so she started the coffeemaker and sat down on the stool.

"I bet you get all kinds of things in here."

"I do. But mainly it's just a lot of the same conditions that we see as people age. Blood pressure, diabetes, heart disease. My goal here is to help people live the longest life they can, but feel good doing it. If I put them on a bunch of medications, they'll just be miserable with side effects."

Zach was quiet. "I don't know if I would agree with that necessarily."

"Really?"

"Well, modern Western medicine saves lives every day. Scientists come up with innovative medications all the time. Are you saying that those shouldn't be used here?"

"Of course not. Look, if you break your leg, you need Western medicine. You need to go to a hospital. Yoga will not help that. But, if you have high blood pressure, I think it's worth trying meditation, yoga, a change in diet, and things like that before you put somebody on a powerful medicine."

He shrugged his shoulders. "I guess you're right. I can see both sides of that. I just know that some-times people need medicine before any of these other remedies are going to work, if they even do. I guess I don't believe in a lot of that woo-woo stuff."

"Well, I'm going to convert you. I'm going to show you how that woo-woo stuff can change lives, even when someone is older."

He reached out his hand and shook hers. "You've got yourself a deal."

CHAPTER 4

MAMIE WALKED ALONG THE BEACH, HER FEET DIGGING into the wet sand. She hadn't lived near a beach before, so this was a delightful change of pace. Even though she'd visited California many times during her life as a tabloid reporter, she hadn't lived along the ocean. It had been far too expensive, even back then.

She wanted to love the quiet pace of Wisteria Island, but her experience in life had been that when things were peaceful, bad things were coming. She always felt like the other shoe was about to drop. Her way around it was to dig for the drama. Find it before it found her. Thankfully, she'd been able to turn that into a successful career for decades... until everyone decided she was "too old".

Mamie felt left behind by the world of media she

helped create. Younger people came in and filled her shoes, full of the knowledge of new technology that she hadn't been able to keep up with. Before she knew it, they were throwing her a "retirement party" she didn't ask for or want.

With her son in another country and her daughter not speaking to her, she was left on her own for a couple of years, living in an apartment near Atlanta, wishing she had a life again. She'd tried to get a job as a local newspaper reporter, but no one would hire a woman in her seventies to do such an active job.

It wasn't like she needed to work. She had been great with her finances over the years, so she had plenty saved to keep her going for the rest of her life. Plus, she had her retirement check and Social Security. But she'd longed for activity, drama, something to do. That's when she saw the article about Wisteria Island. If she was going to be alone for the rest of her life, she figured she might as well be alone with a bunch of other old people who'd basically been abandoned by the world, too.

Nothing had prepared Mamie for the day when she became obsolete. She hadn't truly expected to be marginalized just because she was getting old. All those years of working and contributing to society seemed pointless now. Once she hit sixty, people started looking at her differently, like she had nothing of value to give anymore.

There were times she envied elderly people in Asian countries where she heard they were revered. She certainly didn't feel revered.

When she'd had children, she had always assumed her older years would be spent with them surrounding her, a bunch of grandchildren running around at her feet. She thought she'd be in her kitchen wearing an apron while baking cookies with little ones who idolized her. Instead, she had a son who was across the world, and she had a daughter who hated her. She hadn't even met her new grand-daughter. In fact, she only knew about her from Facebook friends who told her.

As Mamie replayed her life and everything that was wrong with it, she continued walking down the beach, the water lapping at her toes. The sun would set in a couple of hours, so she had to make sure to get back to her cottage by then. Plus, she didn't want to miss dinner. She had many more questions for Dorothy.

She came upon an outcropping of rocks on the sand and considered turning back, but her curiosity got the better of her. She wanted to see what was on the other side. After all, the island was her home now. She deserved to explore every part if she wanted to.

She walked into the water a bit and around the edge of the rocks, choosing not to climb over it. Her balance wasn't what it used to be. As she turned to look back at the beach, she was astounded by what she saw. Over a dozen naked senior citizens were laid out before her. She thought about turning back, but this was just too good to pass up.

"Hello there!" a man said, walking up to her. He was naked as a jaybird, so she refused to look down.

"Hi. Hope I'm not interrupting something?"

He chuckled. "I'm Peter, and we're the Wisteria Island Nudist Society, or WINS for short."

"I had no idea this was offered on Wisteria Island," she said, laughing.

"Well, we keep to ourselves and are only out here certain hours of the day so as not to offend anyone. You can escape to the street that way if you'd like."

Mamie, always up for a little excitement, shook her head. "No, I wouldn't dream of it. Where do I toss these clothes?"

He grinned. "You're going to join us, then?"

"Of course! When in Rome, right?" she said as she walked toward the group, unbuttoning her floral blouse as she went.

Danielle sat at Bennett's desk, staring down at the mounds of files and paperwork. She needed to help him organize his life because this was giving her anxiety.

"Okay, you said the blue folder?" she asked as she sorted through the stack.

"Light blue. Not dark blue," he responded. She loved seeing his face on video chat, but she could tell he was stressed.

"Here it is. What did you need from it?"

"Can you send me a picture of the contract inside? And I think I wrote Melvin's phone number on the inside of the folder."

"You need a better filing system, Bennett," she said, rolling her eyes. She used her phone to take a picture of the contract pages and sent them over before texting the phone number to him.

"I know, I know. Naomi has been on me for months about it."

"Where is she, anyway?" Danielle didn't mind stepping in, but she had patients meeting her at the office soon and wasn't expecting a side trip to Bennett's office.

"She had to go to the mainland for a doctor's appointment today. I think she said an x-ray on her knee. She hurt it playing tennis with Morty the other day."

Danielle chuckled. "He'll run you all over that court with his little legs. He's fast!"

Bennett smiled, but only slightly. She could see he was tired and emotionally drained. The long drive had been hard for him, and then when he got to his great aunt's house, she was worse than he imagined.

"I miss you," he said, looking into the camera. She could see just how pained he was.

"I miss you too. How is your aunt?"

"She's holding her own. She's always been a tough old bird. I think she knows I'm here. I've spent a bunch of time just sitting and holding her hand. I hate she won't be a part of my life soon."

"She'll always be a part of your life. You'll feel her spirit forever, and the things you're doing on Wisteria Island will be done in memory of her."

"How are things going with Zach?"

"Pretty good. He's getting the lay of the land. He got to meet some of the residents and we've treated a few patients together. I think he'll be a great addition to the island."

"Are you two getting along okay?"

"Of course! I'm a professional. I get along with everyone. I've worked with doctors who had horrendously large egos before, and Zach really doesn't. He's open to hearing new ideas, and we've got some big plans."

"Oh really? What kind of plans?"

"Just different things to add to the health fair, and maybe we will even work on getting some new equipment to the island if our boss allows it."

Bennett chuckled. "We'll talk about it once I review the end-of-year budget. Listen, I heard something on the news about a weather pattern forming. It's likely to miss us, but you might want to keep tabs on it since I'm not there."

"Absolutely. At least with hurricanes, we'll have plenty of notice if we need to vacate the island. Is there a plan in place for that?"

"Somewhat. A lot of it really depends on what kind of situation it is. We have partnerships with hotels on the mainland to take our residents, but that would depend on whether they are full at the time."

"What about a boat? Ours isn't big enough to get everyone to the mainland."

"More friends on the mainland to help us if needed."

"Have you ever had a hurricane hit here?"

"Not while we've been here, but that doesn't mean it can't happen. We are on an island, after all. I'm pretty confident in the way we built our structures, though. I invested a lot of money in the buildings on Wisteria Island. Our big structures have concrete reinforced walls, specially designed roofs and other features to make them able to withstand high winds."

"What about the cottages?"

He chuckled. "Well, yours would probably float out to sea, but the newer ones are better. That's why we have many on stilts and more rounded structures, plus a lot of reinforcements in the walls."

She smiled at him. "You really put a lot of thought and money into this island."

"I did, but I'd still prefer to evacuate if an actual hurricane is heading toward us. No need to be heroes."

"I'll watch the news tonight and see what they're saying. You just focus on your great aunt and soak up these moments with her, okay?"

"I love you."

"I love you too."

~

"I finally figured out my ensemble for the fashion show," Morty said, bursting through the door of the clinic. He almost sent Danielle's heart into fibrillation.

"Geez, Morty! You scared me to death," she said, holding her hand to her chest.

"Well, the fashion show is tonight, and I'm just

fluttering all over town, trying to get my act together!"

She'd never seen Morty in such a frenzy. "It's just a fashion show. Why does it have you so riled up?"

He fell into one of the waiting room chairs in his most dramatic flair, throwing his head back and putting the back of his hand over his forehead. "It's an awful memory. I just don't know if I can bring myself to relive it."

She sat down next to him, sure this story would be long and detailed. "What happened?"

"Well, it was way back in college, you see," he said, sitting up and looking at her, his eyes large. "We had one of those fashion shows where the boys dressed in drag and the girls dressed like men."

"I've literally never heard of a fashion show like that."

He shrugged his shoulders. "I can't help that you've led a very dull life, honey. Anyway, Oscar Reynolds was the most popular guy in our whole dorm. All the ladies loved him. He had a date every night of the week."

"Morty, I have patients coming soon. Can you get to the point?"

"I just had to beat Oscar because he was… in a word… a jackass. Pardon my French. I have more flair in my pinky finger than he had in his whole body! I went all over town, from high end boutiques to thrift stores, trying to find the perfect ensemble to blow his snobby butt back to Martha's Vineyard where his family was from. I spent all of my rent money to do it, and old Mr. Vickers, my landlord, just about kicked me out!"

"And?"

"I had the perfect outfit. I mean, darlin', this get-up was going to win me the hundred dollar prize and the title of Mr. Fashion King."

"Wait. You're telling me you did all of this for a hundred bucks and a goofy title?" Danielle couldn't help but giggle at that.

"A hundred dollars back then was good money, and I'm a competitor. You should've seen me back then. I was something to behold! Things didn't sag like they do now."

"I think you look great, Morty. But, please, get to the point of the story."

"Right. So, the night of the fashion show, I put my clothes and shoes in the locker room and went to say hello to my fans."

"Your fans?"

"The ladies loved me, too. I helped all of them with makeup and fashion choices. Some of those girls were homely!"

"Keep going…"

"When I went back to the locker room, my clothing was gone! All that was sitting there was a pair of smelly old tennis shoes with Oscar's name on them. Next thing I know, that jerk won the whole thing, and I never saw my stuff again! I ended up sitting in the locker room crying all night."

"Oh, Morty, that's a horrible story. I'm so sorry. Did you report it to anyone?"

He smiled slightly and shook his head. "No, dear. Back in those days, I was considered an oddball, so to speak. Nobody cared what I thought. I was too much for them."

"I hate that for you. I'm glad times have changed a lot since then, Morty. Wisteria Island wouldn't be the same without your flair!"

"Thank you, Dani girl. Still, I plan to keep my outfit under lock and key tonight. I plan to win this thing!"

"What are you doing for the talent competition?"

He smiled. "That part's a surprise. You'll have to wait and see!" Morty quickly stood up and trotted toward the door. "See you tonight!"

"Good luck!" Danielle called as he opened the door and quickly scurried down the sidewalk.

Mamie sat across from Dorothy, her eyes wide. "And he flirted with you?"

"All the time. That movie set was awful. I kept

fending off his advances, and he kept trying to touch my derriere." Mamie couldn't believe the scoop she was getting. Back in her days of tabloid reporting, this would've been a big story. Dorothy had just spilled the beans about one of the biggest stars in Hollywood making unwanted romantic advances back in her heydey. Dylan Howard had been one of the hottest commodities in the entertainment industry back then. Well respected and considered untouchable when it came to gossip, he even had a star on the Hollywood Walk of Fame.

"Did you report it?"

Dorothy stared at her. "You know how it was in those days, Mamie. Women couldn't speak up like they do now. I would've lost that job, and it was one of my most popular movies."

"Have you ever told anyone?"

"No. What's the use now? He died twenty years ago. It would only hurt his kids and grandkids now."

"Wouldn't you feel better if everyone knew he wasn't the perfect guy they all thought he was?"

She curled her lip upward. "What difference would it make? Life has moved on, and it can't ever be undone."

"I suppose so," she said.

"Well, I'd better get to my appointment with Danielle. She wants to check my blood pressure. It was up a bit at our last appointment."

"Good luck. I'll see you at the fashion show tonight?"

Dorothy nodded. "I wouldn't miss it. Morty would kill me."

Mamie laughed and waved as Dorothy left the cafe. They had enjoyed eating lunches together for the last few days, and Mamie felt like she was actually making a friend. She hadn't had many genuine friends in her life, mostly because nobody really trusted her with their personal stories. That had been a smart idea since Mamie loved a story more than she cared about friendships, or at least that's how she'd spent most of her adult life.

She opened her laptop that she always carried in her oversized tote bag and stared at a blank page. She'd always hated a blank page. They looked much better filled with word pictures, poetic prose, and juicy gossip.

Not writing all the time made her feel like a part of her was missing. She needed something to do aside from playing bingo and eating sandwiches. Then it came to her.

Mamie's Musings

She typed the phrase at the top of the page and smiled. She would start her own digital tabloid all about Wisteria Island, and the world would take notice of her again as she regaled them with stories of its residents. It was sure to be a hit!

CHAPTER 5

Danielle smoothed the back of Morty's jacket and patted his shoulders. "You look fabulous!"

He spun around, a dramatic look on his face. "I know."

Danielle laughed. She showed way too much favoritism toward Morty, but she couldn't help herself. He felt like family to her, and the fact that he'd been abandoned by his own made her feel protective of him. This fashion show was the most important thing in his life right now, and she just had to root for him to win. Of course, in public, she tried to appear impartial, but it was likely that everyone knew how she felt.

"I can't believe you talked me into this," Zach said, walking up behind Danielle. He was staring at a stack of blue note cards and looked like he was sweating a little more than he should've been.

"You'll do fine," she said, picking a piece of lint off Morty's jacket.

"Why can't you do it?"

"Because I'll be helping everyone get on stage at the right time."

"When is Bennett coming back?"

"His great aunt passed last night, so there's the funeral and so forth. It'll be a few more days, I'm sure."

"Sorry to hear that," he said, still staring at the cards.

"Sorry that she died or sorry that he's not here to be the emcee?" she asked, smiling at him.

"Can I say both and not sound terrible?"

"Can ya'll pay more attention to me, please?" Morty asked, staring at them.

"What do you need now? You're all dressed and ready to wow the crowd," Danielle said.

"I need a glass of whiskey is what I need," he said, his southern drawl thick as molasses.

She patted his shoulder. "No, you certainly do not."

"Okay, fine, but I do need to wet my whistle. I'm going to go find a nice glass of sweet tea." He wandered off quickly, leaving Zach and Danielle in his dust.

"He's quite a character, isn't he?"

"Always," she said.

"You know, this is one of the craziest places I've ever been. I tried to describe to my mother on the phone last night, and I couldn't do it justice. I think she fears I'm working at the loony bin."

Danielle looked around the community center, wondering where Morty ran off to, before she sat down at one of the round tables. Zach joined her shortly thereafter and looked back down at the cards.

"My mother was sure I'd lost it when I came to work here. She tried everything to get me to go back home and resume my career."

"Why didn't you?"

"A few reasons, actually. I knew the residents needed me, and honestly, I realized I needed them. Plus, Bennett and I started getting serious."

He smiled. "What's that like? Dating your boss?"

"It doesn't feel like I'm dating my boss. Bennett never makes it feel that way."

"You don't worry about your job if things… don't go well?"

She laughed. "Not really."

"I guess I'm more jaded than you are," he said, making a change on one of the cards with a black pen he took from his shirt pocket.

"Oh, yeah?"

"I had a good friend who dated his boss and ended up losing his job. Took him two years to break back into his career field again."

"There will always be exceptions, I suppose."

"Of course."

"Hey, Danielle. Where's Morty gone off to?" Janice asked. She was wearing her typical attire - pink hair in a bun, a vintage poodle skirt and a white button up dress shirt with the collar turned up. She wasn't even taking part in the fashion show. This was just how she dressed most days.

"He went to get some sweet tea. Honestly, I think he needed a little time to relax before the show. What's up?"

"He asked to borrow my pink scarf," she said, holding up something gaudy.

"Oh. Well, you can leave it with me if you'd like. I should see him again soon."

She tossed it onto the table. "Here ya go. I've got to run. I promised Dorothy I'd help her get dressed."

Danielle was happy to hear Dorothy was at least making some friends. She worried about her, but she finally seemed to be settling in and trusting people.

"This show is going to be the death of me," Danielle said, laughing. "I'd better go find Morty."

"And I had better practice my lines again. Talk about being thrown right into the fire."

She reached up and squeezed his shoulder. "I know you'll rise to the occasion."

"Wow! What a night of fashion and talent we've had," Zach said, smiling in front of the crowd. Danielle was impressed at how he'd handled the evening. He could easily get a gig as a talk show host if the whole doctor thing didn't work out. "Our judges have tallied up the votes, and I have the runner-up and the winner right here inside this envelope. Maybe my trusty assistant could help me up here?"

Danielle rolled her eyes from the front row. Her feet were killing her after a day of treating patients and running all over the community center, but she stood up once again and met him on the small stage. She could see Morty and the other contestants off in the wings, anxiously awaiting the results.

"So, I'm going to announce the runner-up, and I think it's only fair if our beloved island nurse announces the winner. Sound good?" The audience cheered, and Danielle feared they'd all had too much wine. Zach opened the envelope and smiled. "Our runner-up this year is… Dorothy Monroe!"

Dorothy appeared from the side of the stage as everyone clapped. Danielle gave her a hug, although it was a prickly one since Dorothy wasn't the most affectionate person she'd ever met. Zach handed Dorothy the smaller of the two trophies, and she smiled and waved at the audience like she'd won an Oscar before disappearing into the backstage area again.

He handed the envelope to Danielle, and she was nervous. This year, they'd had more entries than ever, at least according to Gladys. She seemed to know everything about the island's history.

"Wow, I'm so nervous," Danielle said, as her hands shook a bit. She pulled the winner's card from the envelope and slowly opened it. A smile spread across her face. "The winner is... Morty!"

Like a spastic little bird, Morty came flying out of the side stage area, and he seemed to float on air. He accepted his trophy - a gaudy gold thing with a metal palm tree protruding from the top - with more glee than Danielle had seen in a while.

"Oh, my goodness!" he said, bumping Zach away from the microphone stand and taking it for himself. "I just cannot believe this! I want to thank the judges, Dr. Zach and Danielle, Bennett even though he isn't here..."

Danielle continued listening to his list of people he wanted to thank, which included the company who made his hairspray, his long-since-dead parents and his favorite childhood dog, Elvis, who'd listened to all his hopes and dreams growing up. When

Morty was finally done, Zach told everyone good-night, and they started dispersing.

"Congratulations, Morty!" Danielle said, hugging him. Morty grinned like a Cheshire Cat.

"Can you even believe it?" He held the trophy in the air, watching it twinkle under the lights. "This is going right on my bedroom dresser so I can see it every morning!"

"So happy for you," Zach said, squeezing his shoulder. Morty looked up at him and smiled.

"Thank you, Dr. Zach."

"Well, I'm exhausted," Danielle said, sighing. It wasn't even eight o'clock yet, and she was fighting back yawns. Was it possible she was becoming an older person who ate dinner at five o'clock and wanted to be in bed right after the sun went down? What had her life become?

"Same here. I'm going to peel these clothes off, open a bottle of bubbly and take a hot bath," Morty said. "Goodnight, ya'll!" He trotted away, obviously delighted with himself.

"That's one happy man right there," Zach said, laughing. "Can I walk you home?"

"I have the golf cart, remember?"

"Oh, that's right. Can I drive you home then?"

"You have the early shift tomorrow, don't you?"

"Yep."

"It actually makes more sense for you to drive me

home and take the golf cart with you. That way you can get to the clinic easier in the morning."

Zach laughed. "It's not a long walk, Danielle. I'll be fine tomorrow."

"Listen, in the early morning, you will not want to walk. I'll be in before lunch, and my cottage is closer to the clinic, anyway."

He shrugged his shoulders. "Fine. If you're sure you don't need it tomorrow."

They walked outside and climbed into the golf cart. "Do you know how to drive this?"

He turned it on and looked at her, a bemused smile on his face. "I'm a doctor, Danielle. Do you know how much golf I've played during my career? It's practically a requirement. Doctors and politicians must play golf."

She nodded her head. "Good point."

They drove down the road, and Danielle felt the welcome breeze against her face. She loved being near the ocean, especially after being cooped up in the clinic and then the community center all day. But this breeze was stronger than normal, and that reminded her to look at the weather station when she got home. Bennett had asked her to do that a couple of days ago, and she'd gotten distracted with Morty and the fashion show.

"Here we are," Zach said as he pulled up in front of her cottage.

"Do you want to come in for a cup of coffee and some danish?"

"I know you said you're tired. I don't wanna keep you up."

"Well, to be honest, I didn't eat any dinner. I'm starving. The fashion show sort of took over my life tonight."

He laughed. "I didn't eat either. Well, unless you count half of a granola bar at about three o'clock today."

She shook her head. "I don't count that. Come on in. I might even be able to rustle up some actual food."

They got out of the golf cart and walked into the house. Danielle flipped on the lights and closed the door behind them.

"This is a nice little place. I can't believe you said it had to have so much work done to be livable."

She walked toward the kitchen, Zach following behind her. "You wouldn't believe what it looked like. It was a mess. We had to do so much work…" As Danielle flipped on the kitchen light, she felt her foot suddenly get wet. She looked down and noticed at least two inches of water covering most of her kitchen floor. It was obvious that the floor wasn't level because most of it was pooling over near the dishwasher.

"Oh, my gosh! You've got a leak."

She backed out of the kitchen and stared at the floor. "What in the world?"

"Did you happen to run your dishwasher?"

"I turned it on before I left for the fashion show. That created this much water?"

"Looks like you might have a busted pipe." He walked closer, his dress shoes getting completely ruined by the water in the process.

"I can call Darryl, our handyman. Don't ruin your shoes."

He turned around, laughing. "I wear these shoes about once a year, so it's no big deal." He kneeled down and looked inside the cabinet, water pouring out when he opened it. "Yep. You've got yourself a pretty bad plumbing situation here."

"Great. And these floors were just redone."

"If we can get it cleaned up fast enough and repair this issue, I think your floors will dry out fine. You don't happen to have a wet/dry vacuum, do you?"

She put her hands on her hips. "Do you honestly think that's something I would have?"

"No. Text the handyman and ask him if he has one. Meanwhile, do you have some towels I can use to get a handle on this water?"

She nodded, walking down the hallway to the linen closet and grabbing every towel she owned. She saw a shopping trip to the mainland in her future because she would have to replace them quickly.

She carried the stack in and handed it to Zack before texting Darryl. It took him a few minutes, but he responded by letting her know he was heading that way. Thankfully, living on an island meant you didn't have to wait very long for someone to show up at your house. It also meant you couldn't get groceries delivered, so there were definitely were trade-offs. She missed the convenience of that.

"Do you think you can help me a minute? I need you to hold this cabinet door open while I take a look at the pipe." Zach was already covered in water from kneeling on the floor. He looked like he had taken a swim in the ocean.

"Sure," Danielle said as she carefully started walking across the floor. She had removed her nice shoes, but the bottoms of her pant legs were definitely getting soaked. As she got closer, her feet started to slip from under her. Zach stood up quickly, reaching out his arms to try to catch her, but she slipped anyway, pulling him down with her.

Both of them were laughing and writhing around on the floor, trying desperately to help each other up. Before she knew it, both of them were flat on their backs, covered in water, and laughing uncontrollably. None of it was funny, of course, but the ridiculousness of it overwhelmed them both.

"Excuse me, but what on earth is going on here?"

Danielle turned her head and noticed Morty standing in the doorway of the kitchen, one of his hands on his hip and the other holding what appeared to be a bottle of champagne.

"Oh, hey, Morty."

"Do you care to explain why the two of you are laying on the floor together covered in water?" He actually seemed to be more than a little irritated.

"There was a leak. I was trying to fix it, and Danielle was attempting to help me. It did not go well."

Danielle started laughing again. She was exhausted, and this whole situation was way funnier because of it.

"Well, don't ya'll think you should get up?"

"Morty, don't you find this funny?"

"Not particularly. I don't think my friend, Bennett, would find it amusing either."

"I think he would find it pretty comical that we're laying in the floor covered in water. I'm waiting for Darryl to get here to help." Danielle pulled on the cabinet door enough to sit up, reaching out a hand to help Zach do the same. They leaned against the cabinet doors, each of them trying to catch their breath.

"Well, I came here to share a glass of champagne

with my friend to celebrate my win tonight. I can see you're busy."

"Zach brought me home because he's going to need the golf cart in the morning. I invited him in for some coffee and danish, but we walked into several inches of water in the kitchen. And then we fell down."

Zach laughed. "That's about the long and the short of it."

"What a mess," Darryl said, walking in behind Morty.

"I was trying to get it cleaned up a bit, but we had a mishap and fell down instead," Zach said. He slowly pulled himself up to a standing position and reached his hand out to shake Darryl's. "I assume you're the handyman?"

"Yes, sir. For the entire island. And you are?"

"Dr. Zach Emerson. Just started working here on the island few days ago."

"Nice to meet you. I think the first thing we need to do is get this water up. I brought my wet/dry vac."

Danielle got up and made her way into the living room to talk to Morty while Zach and Darryl worked in the kitchen.

"Morty, I hope you know nothing was going on. I'm just friends with Zach. We work together."

Morty didn't crack a smile. "And that's how these things start. Bennett is away. A handsome doctor wrestles in water with you. Before you know it, you and Bennett break up and you leave the island."

She smiled and put her hand on his shoulder. "I think you should be a novelist. That's quite a story you're telling yourself."

"Just be careful. That Dr. Zach is handsome and charming."

"And I love Bennett. That hasn't changed, and it's not going to. Stop worrying."

"You know, I don't think I'm feeling up to that champagne. And you have your hands full here. I'm going to head back to my cottage and take that bath now."

"Okay. I'll see you tomorrow?"

"Of course."

As she watched Morty walk down the front steps and out of sight, Danielle couldn't believe how upset he seemed. Would Bennett have been concerned if he had walked in on that scene? It was innocent, of course, but she had to wonder. Was she crossing the line being friends with her coworker?

CHAPTER 6

MAMIE SAT ON THE DECK OF HER COTTAGE
overlooking the water, her fingers typing away on
her laptop. Life was good. She was enjoying her new
home, and the gossip on the island was plenty. Aside
from Dorothy, she'd learned about so many other
residents. The man who used to be a woman. The
woman who used to be an "escort" in her younger
years. The couple who had rap sheets that included
shoplifting and indecent exposure. The bingo
cheating scandal. The nude beach. So much content
to share with the world!

Of course, she used fake names for most people,
since they weren't famous, anyway. For Dorothy, she
couldn't get around it. She had to use her name.
Otherwise, the story wasn't really a story.

She knew Dorothy would be angry if she ever

found out, but how would she? Most of the residents on the island didn't use computers, and she knew Dorothy knew nothing about them. It seemed harmless enough to get the scoop and have Dorothy be none the wiser.

As she clicked the submit button on her first Mamie's Musings column, she felt like herself again. Being surrounded by scandals for most of her career actually felt like home to her. It wasn't something she said out loud, but it was the truth. She needed drama. She needed gossip. Otherwise, she just felt like an old frump.

Her desire for drama had come at an enormous cost - the relationship with her daughter. She didn't like to think about what happened between them because there was a huge weight of guilt that descended over her when she did. At night, though, when she was trying to go to sleep, she often replayed those events in her mind. The mistakes. The words exchanged with her only daughter.

The irony of Mamie's life was that she desperately wanted close relationships with people, but she pushed them away with her actions. It had happened time and time again for as long as she could remember. Her daughter had been no different.

Connie, her daughter, had waited years to marry. Finding the right man hadn't been easy for her, but when she met Phil, everything changed. Mamie had been so excited for them. Phil was a record producer and a pretty successful one at that. When Mamie found out some dirt on Phil's biggest client, she hadn't been able to contain herself. She told Connie first, which she thought was a good thing.

Connie had begged her, even threatened her, to not release the information, especially not right before her wedding. But Mamie had done it anyway, wrecking their relationship and breaking the trust of her daughter. Thinking she could apologize and make things right, Mamie showed up at the wedding only to be turned away.

That moment had been the most painful of her life. She called, texted, sent letters and finally showed up at Connie's home to apologize. She was turned away. That was two years ago, and the only news about her daughter's life had come from friends who were still connected with her on social media.

As she was about to close her computer, she felt a pang in her heart. She missed Connie. She wanted to know her new granddaughter. Gathering her courage, she opened her email and began to type.

My dear Connie, I know this email will come as a shock to you. You probably don't want to hear from me, and I'm sure you don't care about what's going on in my life, but I hope you'll read this, anyway.

I've moved to a place called Wisteria Island. It's off the coast of South Carolina. This magical place is a retirement community, and I'm really enjoying myself so far. You know it's hard for me to make true friends, but I'm trying. Most of all, I miss you, my daughter.

I know I deserved to be punished for breaking your trust, but how long is my sentence? It's been over two years now, and I need you in my life. Your brother is a world away, and you're my only daughter. My life is getting shorter, and I want to spend the rest of it with you in it. Please, Connie, email me back.

I love you,

Mom

With a tear rolling down her cheek, she deleted the email and stared out over the ocean. Maybe she wasn't as brave as she thought.

Danielle stared at the computer screen as she drank her latte. Having a break between patients meant she got to sit down for a few minutes and rest her aching feet. Wearing heels the night before for the fashion show had reminded her why she liked comfortable shoes.

"It says here that the hurricane is gaining strength and could directly hit us later this week," she said, worry settling in her gut. Zach walked over and looked at the radar, too.

"Wow. That doesn't look good at all. What does Bennett say?"

"I haven't talked to him since yesterday. He had his aunt's funeral and some legal stuff to attend to before he comes back. I'm really worried about this. I think I'll start making some calls to local hotels and see if I can move the residents."

"Good idea. I'm glad to help if you want to give me some numbers."

"Thanks. That would be great."

Between seeing patients, Zach and Danielle started making calls. Most local hotels were booked, but a couple of them agreed to reserve suites to house residents. It still wasn't nearly enough to house everyone, so Danielle hoped the storm would change paths. Still, they couldn't count on that.

"I spoke to The Inn at Seagrove, and they said we could bring ten residents there. They will double them up in rooms, and even convert part of the living room to a sleeping area. But we need to transport them today," Zach said.

"Okay. I'll text Eddie and see about getting the boat ready. It will take a few trips. Why don't we prioritize our least mobile residents?"

They started going through the list of residents, choosing those who would fare better on the mainland. Of course, the hurricane would hit that area too, but at least they weren't completely surrounded by water like Wisteria Island.

A few hours later, Danielle and Zach were standing on the dock, helping the first residents into the boat. Danielle decided to go with them so she could chat with the inn's owners and thank them in person for taking some of the residents. Even though the storm was a couple of days off, it made more sense to be proactive in getting people off the island early.

"You mind seeing the rest of the patients for today?"

Zach shook his head. "It's kind of my job, Danielle. You go on. I'll keep calling hotels and see if we can get any more space."

"Thanks. See you later."

As the boat zipped away, Danielle couldn't help but feel worry start to overwhelm her. What would happen to Wisteria Island if the hurricane made a direct hit? Was Bennett going to get back in time? Would they be able to ride out a hurricane?

These were the thoughts that consumed her mind until the boat finally docked outside The Inn At Seagrove. It was a beautiful place, from what she could tell. There was a beach area and a large outdoor deck with tons of tables. This part of Seagrove was called an island, but it was attached to the mainland and had more protection than Wisteria Island could offer.

"Welcome!" a man said as they pulled up to the dock. He was tall, with slightly messy, dirty blond hair, and looked more like a surfer than an inn owner. "I'm Dawson."

Danielle reached out her hand as he helped her out of the boat. "Danielle Wright. I'm the nurse over on Wisteria Island."

"Oh, I think my wife, Julie, has mentioned you."

"I didn't know Julie was your wife. Small world, I suppose."

"Well, it's great to have ya'll here. Come on inside."

Everyone slowly got out of the boat, with Jeremy helping them. Eddie had stayed back on the island after coordinating the boat transport for them. Danielle assisted each resident, helping them get onto the dock as Jeremy and Dawson carried their bags.

"This is a lovely place," Danielle said as they walked toward the front door.

"It's been in my family for a long time."

They walked inside, and Danielle was impressed by the historical decor. She'd always loved antiques, and this place was full of them. A woman appeared from the back of the house.

"Welcome to The Inn At Seagrove. I'm Lucy."

"Nice to meet you, Lucy," Danielle said, shaking her hand.

"Lucy is our amazing cook, and she keeps this place running smoothly. She will show everyone to their rooms and get you anything you need."

As Lucy started taking residents upstairs, Danielle felt a small wave of relief wash over her. At least some of the residents had a place to go. What they'd do about everyone else was beyond her at the moment.

"Hurricanes are stressful," she said, sighing.

"They are, but I've been through a few in my life. My best advice is to try not to panic, and know that they are unpredictable and could change course at the last minute. You prepare, and then you wait."

"What will you do to prepare here?"

"We use a lot of sandbags down near the water, and we've got hurricane shutters installed. I watch the weather closely, and if we need to move further inland, I can call in some favors. Don't you worry. I'll keep your residents safe, Danielle."

She was grateful to hear that. So much was on her shoulders without Bennett around, and she was feeling the weight of it all today. There was a ticking time clock in her head, and she wished it would slow down and give her more time.

～

Morty sat across from Dorothy, a pile of chicken salad on the plate in front of him. "I love when they put pineapple in it, don't you?"

She stared at him. "Pineapple in chicken salad? That's disgusting."

He rolled his eyes. "I bet you don't like pineapple on pizza either, do you?"

"Were you raised by wolves?"

The two of them ate lunch together most days, Dorothy poking fun at him and Morty enjoying the back-and-forth of their arguments. Being around a bunch of old people, as he called them, sometimes bored him beyond tears. But Dorothy challenged him, and he'd been a big fan of hers for years.

"I was raised by a shoe salesman and a homemaker."

"That sounds dull," she said, taking a sip of her sweet tea.

"Who were you raised by?"

"My father was an architect. He designed skyscrapers in New York City. My mother was a model. She immigrated here from Russia when she was sixteen years old."

Morty grumbled. "Well, my mom could make a mean peach cobbler."

"Do you know the Kramer building near Times Square? My father designed that."

Morty thought for a moment. "I've only been to

New York City a couple of times. I don't remember that building."

"Look it up on your little phone. It's beautiful. My father's name was Nicholas Monroe."

Morty pulled out his phone, quickly losing interest in talking about buildings and what their parents did for a living. He would much rather talk about fashion and the latest island gossip. Still, he pulled his phone from his pocket and typed in the words to find a picture of the building.

"This?" he said, holding up the phone to show a picture of a tall building against the New York City skyline.

"That's the one. We lived just a few blocks from there in a lovely brownstone."

"We lived in a cottage near the Baptist Church," Morty muttered under his breath. He'd always wanted to be rich and famous, but instead he spent his life dressing like he was rich and famous.

Just as he was about to put his phone back in his pocket, he noticed Dorothy's name in the search results.

"What are you looking at now?" she asked, taking a bite of her salad.

"Um..."

"Um what? I swear those phones are the bane of our society."

"Dorothy, I don't know how to tell you this."

"Tell me what?"

He swallowed loudly, knowing a can of worms was about to open right in the middle of their table. "There's a story here about you."

"Oh that? I was a Hollywood actress for decades, Morty. I'm sure there are lots of old stories about me." She went back to eating her salad.

"No, this one was written yesterday."

"Yesterday?"

"And it appears it was written by… Mamie."

"Mamie? You mean the new lady on Wisteria Island?"

"The very same one." He stared down at his phone, quickly reading the story.

"What does it say, Morty?"

He cleared his throat. "She's claiming a certain well-known, deceased Hollywood actor made advances toward you."

Dorothy's face went pale, and her mouth fell open, a little piece of lettuce still protruding from her bottom teeth. Not a great look, but Morty decided not to mention it.

"Oh, my gosh…"

"Is this true?"

She paused for a long moment. "Yes, it's true. But I told her in strictest confidence. I thought we were becoming friends."

Morty felt horrible for Dorothy. This was a big

story, even all these years later. Here she was, trying to live a quiet life in her older years, and now she was being thrust into the limelight once again.

He looked back down at his phone and clicked on Mamie's name, which took him to a new search. It only took a few clicks to find out the truth.

"Wow."

"What now?"

"Did Mamie ever tell you she was a tabloid reporter?"

Dorothy looked shocked. "What? No! Of course not. Why that little…"

"She tricked you."

"If I didn't have arthritis in my hands, I'd strangle her!" Dorothy said loudly. People at other tables turned around and looked their way.

"Maybe hold it down just a smidge, dear."

She pushed her salad to the center of the table and laid her forehead against the tablecloth. "I can't believe this. I never wanted this story to get out."

"I'm so sorry, Dorothy. Is there anything I can do?"

She sat up slowly, one eyebrow hiked so high that it almost went into her hairline. "Do you have a gun?"

Morty put his hand on his chest. "Lord no!"

She sighed. "Then I don't know a way you can

help me. But when I see that woman again, it's going to be ugly."

Danielle stood on the dock, waving as Jeremy and Zach arrived back on the island. It had been a long day of shuttling residents from the island to the mainland. Finding housing for so many people in such a short timeframe was almost impossible. Hotels were already full, and they had officially run out of places to take them. Thankfully, the residents with the worst health conditions or who had mobility issues were safely tucked away all over Seagrove and the greater Charleston area.

"How'd it go?"

"I got a date!" Zach said, laughing, as he stepped onto the dock.

"Excuse me?"

"Yeah. I took a group to the Lassiter Hotel, and I met the front desk clerk. Turns out we went to the same high school, although in different years. Anyway, she asked me out."

"*She* asked *you* out?"

He poked out his chest. "Yep, she sure did. There's a ballroom dancing bar she wants to try."

Danielle giggled. "I don't think those words go together. Ballroom dancing bar?"

"Apparently it's a new trend. The only problem is, I don't have a clue how to ballroom dance."

They started walking toward the golf cart. "Ballroom isn't the actual dance, you know. There are types of ballroom dancing like the waltz, the foxtrot, the tango..."

"You're stressing me out," he said, climbing inside of the golf cart as Danielle slid behind the steering wheel.

"Why did you agree to this if you don't know how to dance?"

"First off, I agreed because she's cute. Second, I know how to dance. I've got good rhythm. I just don't know how to do any of the *ballroom* dances."

Danielle started driving. "My mom made me take ballroom dance classes as a kid."

"She made you take ballroom dance lessons? Why?"

"My mother believes in being 'high class', for lack of a better phrase. I guess she thought that if I knew how to ballroom dance, I could snag a rich man one day."

Zach laughed. "Well, you did kind of snag a rich man."

"True. But it wasn't my ballroom dancing that did it. And I didn't care if Bennett was rich or not."

"I was just making a joke."

"I get it. I'm sure a lot of people think that I'm

with Bennett because he's wealthy, but that has nothing to do with it. I've never needed a man's money."

"I believe you. Now, back to this whole ballroom dancing thing. How much would I have to pay you to give me a few lessons?"

She pulled up in front of the clinic and leaned back against the seat. "Let me think," she said, tapping her fingers together in front of her face. "I really don't want to see Mrs. Solomon this week. She's got this foot fungus thing. Oh, and there's Mr. Eason. That man always hits on me. He tried to touch my butt the last time he was in. And I don't want to have to do all the accounting for the month."

"Okay, so if I do foot fungus, Mr. Butt Toucher and the spreadsheets, you will teach me a few dances?"

"I suppose so. I mean, maybe you'll fall in love with that hotel clerk, and I will be able to say that it was all because I taught you the foxtrot."

Zach chuckled. "Great. How about we start tonight? We can watch the weather and you can teach me some fancy footwork. I'll bring pizza, and we can meet at your place around seven?"

"Let's shoot for six because I like to go to bed early."

"Okay, Grandma. Six o'clock it is. Now we'd better get inside and see some of these patients."

CHAPTER 7

MORTY SAT AT THE TABLE, WATCHING DOROTHY'S FACE as she waited for Mamie to show up in the cafeteria. He felt like there was going to be some sort of rumble. It was like a version of West Side Story, and he was just waiting for Dorothy to stand up and start snapping her fingers.

"Where is she?" Dorothy said through clenched teeth. She spent the whole day wandering around the island looking for Mamie. Somehow, the woman had managed to stay out of sight.

"I'm sure she'll be here. Everybody has to eat at some point."

"Do you think she's hiding from me on purpose?"

"Maybe. She should."

Morty craned his head around and noticed Danielle and Zach come into the cafeteria. He still wasn't totally sure about those two. They seemed to be awfully chummy, and he couldn't wait for Bennett to get back.

"I'm going to go get my plate," Dorothy said.

"Okay. I'll save your seat."

He watched her walk up to the line of people to get her bowl of chicken pot pie. It was one of Morty's favorite meals, but tonight he didn't feel nearly as hungry as he normally did. He was worried about the oncoming storm, about Bennett not making it back in time, and about what Dorothy was going to do to Mamie. He didn't like to see blood-shed. It made him queasy just to get his own blood drawn.

"Hey, Morty. Are you going to eat?" Danielle asked, standing there with a smile on her face.

"I see you brought your boy toy." He crossed his arms and turned his head away from her.

"Now, Morty, you know that Dr. Zach is just an employee of the island, like I am. You have to stop saying things like that because they're not true."

"I just think you're getting awfully friendly with him."

Danielle sat down across from him. "I've spent my whole life looking for my soulmate, and Bennett is that person as far as I'm concerned. I'm just friends with Zach."

"I hope you're not lying to yourself," he said. "Are you eating?"

"Actually, no. We just came by to check on everybody before we eat a pizza at my place."

Morty stared at her. "Seriously?"

"I'm teaching him some dance moves for a date he has."

"Oh, girl, that's the oldest line in the book. There's no date. He just wants to spend an evening dancing with you."

Danielle shook her head. "No, that's not the case. Zach isn't interested in me."

"I'm going to have an anxiety attack," he said, sighing. "What are we doing about this whole hurricane situation?"

"Well, unfortunately, there aren't any more places to send people. We had to prioritize those who have concerning health conditions or mobility issues, and we've moved those people off the island. But the rest of us are going to ride everything out here together."

"I've never been in a hurricane, so it's giving me a lot of stress."

"I understand, but Bennett built this island to withstand a hurricane. There are buildings that have been created solely for this purpose. I'm sure we're going to be fine."

"I hope you're right."

"Well, I'd better get going. Make sure to eat

something. You don't want your blood sugar getting too low."

Morty watched as Danielle walked back over to Zach and then left the cafeteria. He still thought she was making a mistake spending so much time with him. Before he had a chance to think more about it, Dorothy sat down across from him again.

"You should go get a bowl before they run out. This stuff is like gold in here."

"I will, but I... Oh no. There's Mamie."

Dorothy turned to see Mamie walking through the cafeteria door, a big smile on her face as she greeted several people. Then she saw Dorothy, pointed and started walking towards her, grinning.

"Hey! I was hoping to see y'all here. Let me go get my food and I'll join you."

Dorothy stood up, her eyes furrowed together in an angry expression. She walked a few inches forward until her face was close to Mamie's, although Mamie was much shorter.

"I cannot believe you would have the gall to think that you're going to sit with us."

Mamie stepped back, a look of confusion on her face. "What on earth is going on? We always sit together."

"You think I want to even look at you after what you did?"

"What I did? What did I do?"

Morty pulled his phone out of his pocket and held it up to Mamie. "Does this ring any bells?"

Mamie took the phone from his hand and stared at the screen. She looked like a frozen ice sculpture, not moving or blinking for a few moments. The blood seemed to drain from her face. "Where did you get this?"

"It doesn't matter where we got it. Why did you write this? And why did you publish it on the Internet?" Morty felt his face getting flush as he thought about how much the whole fiasco had hurt his friend, Dorothy.

"I didn't think anyone would see it," she stammered before Morty swiped the phone from her hand.

"You took something I told you in confidence, and you put it on the World Wide Web for all the world to see," Dorothy said, her eyes filling with tears. Morty had never seen her shed a tear before. She was one of the strongest women he'd ever met, and she never let anyone see her sweat. For a moment, he thought of telling her no one called it the World Wide Web anymore, but he thought better of it.

"Dorothy, I'm so sorry. I didn't think anyone would read my blog. I was just writing…"

"Liar!" Dorothy yelled. Tables of people turned around, all of them staring at the normally quiet

Dorothy.

"I don't know what else to say. I'll take it down…"

"It's already out there. News outlets have picked it up," Morty said, staring at his phone.

"Excuse me, folks, I'm not sure what's going on here, but can we please hold it down a bit?" Naomi, Bennett's assistant, walked over and touched Dorothy on the arm.

"Sorry, Naomi. I didn't mean to cause a problem. I'll just go," Mamie said, turning and walking toward the door.

"Oh, sure! Run off and hide. You're a coward and a terrible friend!" Dorothy shouted as Mamie disappeared.

"Dorothy, are you okay?" Naomi asked.

"No, I'm not. That… woman… and I use that term loosely… she put gossip online about me…"

Naomi bit her bottom lip. "Well, that explains a lot."

"Explains what?" Morty asked.

"We've been getting calls for Dorothy all afternoon. Interview requests."

Dorothy slid down into her chair and groaned. "I came to this island to get away from my old life and build something new, just for me. In one fell swoop, that woman - that tabloid reporter - put me right back in the limelight again."

"We need to ask Bennett to send her packing,"

Morty said, reaching over and rubbing Dorothy's arm.

"Don't worry, Dorothy. We won't let any of those reporters get to you. You're safe on Wisteria Island. I hope you know that," Naomi said in a reassuring voice. "Bennett will be back soon, and we'll figure out what to do from here. Okay?"

Dorothy said nothing, but laid her head on the table. Morty smiled and waved to Naomi as she walked away. His beloved Wisteria Island seemed to be in jeopardy between the storm, Mamie causing trouble for Dorothy, and his worries about Bennett and Danielle. These people were his family, and he was going to do anything he could to keep his beloved community together.

"Okay, one more piece and then that's it," Danielle said, eating her third piece of pizza. She knew she shouldn't have another one, but pizza was her favorite food.

"Don't you know about the rule of pizza?" Zach asked, leaning back against one of the Adirondack chairs on her deck.

"What's that?"

"You cannot eat too much pizza. It is specifically

made to be eaten in unlimited amounts, and there are no calories."

She looked over at him, taking another bite of her slice. "No calories, huh? Where did you learn that?"

He smiled. "Well, you see, I'm a big fancy doctor, and we learned that top secret information in medical school. Since you're just a lowly nurse, you weren't privy to this important information that only doctors are given."

She tossed a piece of crust at him. "A lowly nurse?"

Zach burst into laughter. "I'm kidding, I'm kidding. Stop the assault. Besides, I have nothing but respect and admiration for nurses. They do the real work."

She squinted her eyes. "Are you buttering me up for that dance lesson?"

Zach shrugged his shoulders. "Maybe a little. But, honestly, nurses are heroes. Don't ever let anyone tell you otherwise. Doctors might pay a lot more for schooling, but nurses do the heavy lifting."

"Thanks. I really appreciate you recognizing my profession. Now, I think we should start those lessons. You ready?"

He stood up. "Ready as I'll ever be."

Danielle picked up her phone and chose a playlist

that would work for ballroom dancing. "Let's start with the waltz. That's a pretty simple one."

They stepped into a more open part of the deck, and Danielle opened her arms. Zach took her hands. "Okay, oh wise one, lead me."

"Nope. You have to lead, Zach. You're the man here."

"Oh, right."

"So, as the lead, you want to step forward with your left foot… now move the right… ouch, that was my toe… now close your left foot next to your right foot… ouch, that was my toe again…"

"Sorry. Oh, crud. Sorry again…"

They continued moving around the deck until the song ended, and Danielle had to say Zach got pretty good as the music played. Her toes were hurting, but she considered it a success. They danced the waltz to another song, and he had it down pat by then, so Danielle decided to move onto something a little more difficult.

"That was really good!" she said as she stepped back. "How do you feel?"

"Like a newborn horse who hasn't used its legs yet."

Danielle laughed. "I think they're called foals."

"Anyway, if waltzing was that hard, I don't know how I'll learn the other dances."

"Well, now we're going to try the tango. I think

you'll do great!" She pressed a few buttons on her phone to find the proper music.

"Maybe I should cancel this date, or suggest another place to go. I mean, what woman chooses a ballroom dancing club for a first date?"

She stepped forward and took his hands. "Stop trying to talk yourself out of it, Zach. You obviously like this woman. You can do this!"

"I hope you're right."

"Okay, so the tango is five steps, but it's done to eight counts of music. It goes slow, slow, quick, quick, slow. So, step forward with your left foot… Ouch!"

"Sorry…"

Bennett stepped off the boat and sighed. He was so happy to be back on Wisteria Island. His home. His community.

It was pitch black dark, and normally he never would've had Jeremy pick him up from the mainland so late, but hotels were full due to the impending storm. Plus, he wanted to sleep in his own bed. His trip to Louisiana had been one uncomfortable bed after another.

Mostly, though, he wanted to see Danielle. He wanted to feel her arms wrapped around him and her cheek against his chest. He'd been surprised at just how much he'd missed her.

"Well hello, stranger!" he heard Morty say in his unmistakable voice. He was standing at the other end of the dock, waving a white hankie like one of those women saying goodbye to the men as they went off to war. Morty was a funny guy.

"Hey there! Good to see you." Bennett reached out his hand, but Morty hugged his waist instead. "What are you doing down here so late?"

"Well, we've had some serious drama on this island lately. I was just walking home from Dorothy's house. She's quite a mess right now."

"What happened?"

He waved his hand. "It's a lot to explain, and I know you must be tired. I'll find you tomorrow and give you all the details."

"Actually, I'm going to go see Danielle before I head home."

Morty bit his lip. "Oh, dear."

"Oh dear? What is that supposed to mean?"

"Bennett, I don't know how to say this, but Danielle might've changed a bit since you left…"

"What?"

"I've noticed her spending a lot of time with that new doctor."

"Zach? Of course, she's spending time with him. They work together."

"The other evening, I dropped by her house unannounced and they were laying on the floor together, all tangled up."

He felt his face flush. "What?"

"Danielle said it was nothing, but then I saw them tonight at dinner together. And they left early. She said they were having pizza at her place."

"They didn't eat dinner with the residents?"

"Nope."

"I need to go," Bennett said, walking past Morty and climbing into the golf cart.

"Good luck!" Morty called as Bennett drove toward Danielle's cottage, wondering what he might find.

Bennett pulled up in front of Danielle's cottage and noticed the lights were on inside, but he couldn't see her. As he was walking toward the front door, he heard music. It wasn't the type of music she normally played, but instead sounded like tango music. Not that he'd ever tangoed before, but he'd seen it on TV and movies.

He walked around the side of the cottage and looked up toward the deck. The tiki torches were lit, and in the middle of the deck stood Zach and Danielle, cheeks pressed together as they tangoed from one side to the other. Bennett couldn't believe his eyes.

He watched them for a few moments, and neither spoke a word. They just kept dancing. A part of him - the one with all the testosterone - wanted to run toward Zach and push him off the deck. The other part of him - the one that wanted to keep his girlfriend - kept his feet firmly planted on the sand. Surely there was a logical explanation for what he was seeing.

Bennett had only been gone a few days, and already his girlfriend was in the arms of another man? A more handsome man? A man who shared her passion for medicine? His stomach churned. Maybe it was nerves, but it was possible it was the gas station meatball sub he'd eaten on the long drive home.

The music ended, and Danielle stepped back. "That was amazing!"

Zach laughed. "I'm getting pretty good at this, don't you think?"

She smiled broadly. "Very good. I don't think I've had a better dance partner."

"Oh, come on now. I'm blushing," he said, waving his hand at her. "Hey, do you want to eat that lemon meringue pie now?"

"That sounds awesome," she said before they disappeared into the cottage, shutting the door behind them. Bennett stood there, frozen, his legs unable to move. What did he just witness? And why didn't he speak up? Clear this throat? Instead, he'd let this handsome doctor take his girlfriend back inside for a delectable treat and God knew what else.

Maybe Morty was right. Something was going on, and he didn't like it. Maybe Danielle was planning to dump him and run off with her dancing doctor model-looking hot-and-sexy co-worker.

Sometimes Bennett was amazed at how little having a lot of money had helped him with his self-esteem. If anything, it'd made it worse. He never knew if someone liked him for his personality or the thickness of his wallet. He'd never had those thoughts about Danielle, though. She didn't seem to care a bit about his bank account. That meant if she was planning to break up with him, it was his personality and that was a lot harder to take.

He sucked in a deep breath and blew it out before he walked back to the front of the cottage. Climbing into the golf cart, he got away from the house as quickly as he could. He just needed to go home, get a good night's sleep, and figure this out in the morning. Who was he kidding? There was no way he was getting a good night of sleep after seeing Danielle in Zach's arms.

"So you haven't seen Danielle yet? She doesn't know you're back?" Morty asked before biting into his BLT. Bennett stared off at the water, trying to get some peace from looking at the waves.

"Oh, I saw her. She just didn't see me."

"Don't you think you should go talk to her?"

He sighed. "I will. I'm just being immature for a little bit. Then I'll go act like an adult."

"I enjoy being immature myself. It's a nice break from reality," Morty said, giggling.

"Distract me. Tell me what else has been going on around here."

"Oh Lord. Where do I even begin? Well, first of all, I won the fashion show!"

"I heard. Danielle texted me about that. Congratulations."

"Thanks. I love winning things. Anyway, the other big thing going on has to do with Mamie and Dorothy."

"Mamie?"

"The new resident."

"Oh, that's right. My brain isn't firing on all cylinders today. What happened?"

"Well, it turns out she used to be a pretty famous tabloid reporter," Morty said, leaning over the table. "And she got some rather personal information out of poor old Dorothy and wrote about it on the internet! Well, I happened across the article and had to break it to Dorothy. Naomi says reporters have been calling here trying to get a comment from Dorothy too. It's just the biggest mess!"

"Oh no…"

"Something has to be done. That woman… Mamie… she needs to get off this island or else I do believe Dorothy might drown her or stab her with one of those fancy high heels she owns."

Bennett rolled his eyes. "I think you might be stirring the pot a bit, Morty."

He waved his hand like he was brushing the comment away. "No, I am not. I love Dorothy, and I want her to feel safe here."

"I do too. I'll have to talk to Mamie, get to the bottom of this whole situation."

"She's a snake, so be careful you don't get bit."

"I'll take it under advisement. Now, if you'll excuse me, I need to get over to the clinic and see how my medical staff is doing." Bennett stood and pushed in his chair.

"Good luck, my friend."

CHAPTER 8

Mamie stood on Dorothy's front porch, her hands shaking. She'd been standing there for a good ten minutes, trying to summon the courage to knock. It wasn't in her nature to do apologies. Her line of work had made it where she didn't have to say she was sorry to people very often. Nobody expected high morals from a tabloid reporter.

She was trying to make a new life on Wisteria Island, and it hadn't taken her very long to screw it all up. She knew that if she wasn't careful, she'd spend her older years alone because nobody would want to be around her. She couldn't be trusted, and even she knew that.

There was a part of her that felt like if she broke every story and told every secret, somehow that made her look bigger than she was. More impressive. But what it really did was make her feel alone.

She'd been up all night, thinking about Dorothy but also thinking about her daughter. What kind of woman wrecked her relationship with her only daughter just for the sake of a story? She decided there must be something inherently broken about her that she couldn't maintain relationships with people.

Finally, she allowed her knuckles to tap against the door. There was silence. Dorothy had probably looked out the window and saw it was her. Part of her expected Dorothy might swing the door open and slap her across the face. Or poke her with a steak knife. Or kick her in the shin. She would deserve all of it, of course.

She continued standing there, hoping that Dorothy would let her in. That they could talk. That things could be resolved, and then apologies would be accepted. But nothing happened. Just silence. She didn't even know what she planned to say if Dorothy answered the door. A part of her considered falling to her knees, clasping her hands together in a prayer position and trying to force a few tears. But, alas, she had failed theater in high school and hadn't gotten much better in her older years.

"Why are you standing on my front porch?"

She turned around to see Dorothy standing at the

end of her walkway, arms crossed, a brown paper bag from the grocery store hanging from the crook of her elbow.

"I came to apologize again," Mamie said, walking toward her. Dorothy held up a hand, alerting her to stop.

"I want you to get off my property."

"Dorothy, please just let me explain…"

"There's absolutely nothing to explain. I don't know if you have a mental problem or you're just sociopathic, but anybody who would move to an island full of new people and then immediately try to screw them over has something wrong with them."

Dorothy walked past her, bumping her with a grocery bag as she made her way to the front door.

"I know there's something wrong with me. There's been something wrong with me for many years. It's why I don't even have a relationship with my own daughter."

Dorothy turned around, a look of curiosity on her face. "You did something like this to your own kid?"

"I did. I found out something about one of her husband's clients, and she asked me to keep it to myself. Instead, I publicized it right before their wedding, and I was uninvited. I haven't spoken to her since."

"You need help. What kind of mother does that?"

Without warning, Mamie felt tears welling in her eyes. They started to spill over and run down her cheeks. The warm liquid was something she wasn't quite used to. She was always a "get them before they get me" kind of person, and that didn't lend itself well to crying a lot. She was the one always making other people cry.

"Trust me, I've asked myself that question many times. I was a good mother until I wasn't. I chose my career over my relationship with my daughter, and that's how I ended up alone."

"If you're expecting me to feel sorry for you, you've come to the wrong place," Dorothy said, turning to unlock her door.

"I don't think you should feel sorry for me. I just want you to know that I truly apologize for what I did. I was feeling a little lonely here and like I didn't have a purpose in my life anymore. My purpose has always been my job, and I don't know who I am without that."

Dorothy set down her grocery bag just inside the house and turned around to look at her again. "You know, I could've really been a good friend to you. I understand what you're going through. I was an actress for decades, and when I first came here, I didn't know who I was anymore. Sometimes I still struggle with that. But instead of being my friend and allowing me to support you, you stabbed me in the back. And it's unfortunate that I'm not a very forgiving person. Good luck to you, Mamie. People know who you are now, and you're going to need a lot of luck on this island."

Without another word, she quietly walked into her house and shut the door. Mamie stood there, unsure of what to do next. Maybe she should just move right off the island and find herself some retirement home where nobody spoke to each other, and they had bingo on Tuesday nights. She could eat in one of those crappy little cafeterias where the chocolate pudding had a film over the top. There were many places like that across the country where family members dumped their elderly and never came to visit. Those people didn't deserve a punishment like that, but she did.

Danielle peered into Miss Oliveira's eyes. "They are a little red. Perhaps you are struggling with some allergies. I'm going to prescribe some eyedrops. I want you to use them at least twice a day for the next week and see if it helps, okay?"

"Okay, dear. Thank you so much," she said, squeezing Danielle's hand. It was one of the best parts of her job, the closeness she had developed with her patients.

"Zach is going to get you that prescription while I go check on my next patient. I'll see you in a couple of weeks to follow up, alright?"

Miss Oliveira nodded and smiled sweetly. Today, she had brought Danielle some freshly made tortillas. She planned to have some of those as soon as she got home tonight.

"Hey." She heard the familiar sound of Bennett's voice standing in the doorway between the waiting room and the back of the clinic. Danielle grinned broadly.

"Oh, my gosh! I didn't know you were back!" She ran over to him and hugged him tightly. "I'm so happy you're here. I was worried you might not make it back before the storm hit."

Bennett stepped back a bit and looked at her. "I got in last night."

She tilted her head slightly. "Last night? Why didn't you call me or come by?"

"I was just really tired."

"Oh." It was unlike Bennett to not at least let her know he was back on the island. The closeness they had developed was unlike anything she'd ever experienced with previous boyfriends, so it made her a little nervous that he was acting a bit standoffish this morning.

"I just thought I'd come by and see how every-thing has been going since I've been gone. How is Zach working out?"

"Great. He was the emcee at the fashion show. And he's doing a wonderful job with the patients. They really seem to like him."

"Have you two gotten to spend some time togeth-er?" She thought that was a strange question.

"Well, yes. We've had to work together a lot since you've been gone. We've moved quite a few of the residents off the island to some different locations. Mostly, we've taken turns riding with Jeremy to take them over to the mainland."

"Good. We still have quite a few people here on the island, though. Any plans for them?"

"We've really run out of places for them to stay. I did put in a couple of phone calls today, so I'm just waiting to hear back. But it looks like a lot of us are going to be on this island when the storm hits."

He nodded. "I think we'll be fine. The buildings are fortified, so this is the time I guess we will be testing whether they will hold up or not."

That didn't make Danielle feel great. She wasn't so much worried about herself as she was about her residents. But there was not a whole lot they could do without more places to house them on the mainland.

"Do you want to go grab some lunch? I'd love to

talk to you about everything that has happened here since you left."

He shook his head. "No, I really don't have time today. Trying to catch up on all of my work, you know."

"Oh, okay. Dinner tonight then?"

"I'm sure I'll see you in the cafeteria. Is that where you still eat?"

Again, a very strange question. "Of course it is. That's part of the job, right?"

"Right. Well, I'll see you this evening then."

Without another word, he turned and walked out of the clinic. Danielle felt an emptiness in her gut. She wasn't sure exactly what was going on. Maybe he was still feeling the grief of losing his great aunt, but she had hoped that he would lean on her instead of becoming distant, like he seemed to be right now.

"Hey, are you ready to go in and see Mr. Ellis?" Zach asked, poking his head around the doorway.

"Yeah, I'm coming."

Danielle stood down on the dock as William arrived in his boat. She had the idea last night to call in a favor from her friend in Seagrove. She met William and his new wife, Janine, during her visits over to

Seagrove. In fact, she and Bennett even went on a marsh tour in William's boat.

Last night, while she was laying in bed trying to think of ways to protect the residents, she realized that William had a bigger boat and might be able to cart quite a few of them over to the mainland if she could find somewhere for them to stay.

Thankfully, Janine had come up with the idea of housing them at a home that was being used by two women who were formerly in the foster care system in that area. They were using the house as a place to help current foster kids gain job skills. Thankfully, those kids didn't stay there overnight, so that left some rooms available. William had come today to take ten more of the residents over to Seagrove.

"The water is getting pretty choppy," William said, as he tied up the boat and stepped out.

"Yeah, I can see that. Zach is going to be bringing the residents down here in just a minute. We have a small passenger van, so all of them can be brought at once."

"Are you sure you guys are going to be okay on this island? I'm not sure if we're going to actually have a hurricane or just a really strong tropical storm at this point, but I hate to leave you here."

"We've been watching the weather really care-fully, and we have buildings here that are fortified for hurricanes. There's nowhere else to stay on the mainland. All the hotels are booked."

"Yeah, that's what I've heard. I wish I had more room at my place."

"I think we'll be okay. I really appreciate you coming to get the residents, though. And please thank Celeste and Abigail for me. The fact that they are opening their home like this is truly a miracle for us."

"This island is beautiful. I've never been over here before."

"Yes, it's a special place. Of course, Seagrove is also a wonderful place. We are truly blessed to get to live where we do, aren't we?"

He smiled and nodded. "We are."

A few moments later, Zach arrived in the van. He helped each of the residents out, carrying their bags. Danielle grabbed a few bags, as did William, before helping each of them into the boat. Danielle had offered to ride with William back to Seagrove, but he felt like he could handle it. He had Dawson on the other side, ready to help him transport all the residents over to the home where they'd be staying. Danielle was so happy that she had made friends in Seagrove.

"All right, I'm going to get these folks back across before this water gets any choppier."

"Thanks again!" Danielle called out as the boat started to move away.

"That's a relief. Ten fewer people on the island."

She turned and looked at Zach. "Have you talked to Bennett since he got back?"

"Bennett's back?"

"You didn't know either? He came back last night. And when he came to see me today at the clinic, he was acting awfully strange."

"Grief about his aunt?"

"I don't know. I feel like there's something he's not telling me, and I don't like it one bit."

Mamie sat across from Bennett. She'd only met him briefly once before, but she felt nervous, as if she was sitting in front of her high school principal. Mr. Abernathy had been the most intimidating man, with his tall stature and sharp features. Her fear of him still didn't stop her from getting into trouble and ending up in his office over and over.

"Did you hear me?"

She stared at him. "Sorry. I was lost in thought for a minute."

"Mamie, this is serious. Do you know how many calls we're getting for Dorothy? We've had seven today so far, and it's not even dinnertime yet."

"I know, and I'm so sorry. I've apologized to Dorothy twice now, but she just won't hear me out."

"So, this is her fault?"

She sighed. "No, of course not."

"Look, I've spoken to a few of the residents, and to be honest, they want you off the island. They don't trust you."

"Why would they?"

"We don't allow drama here. This is a safe, loving place, and we work hard to keep it that way."

"I understand. Can I at least stay until the storm passes? I don't have anywhere lined up to go."

He looked at her with compassion in his eyes. "Mamie, I'm not asking you to leave, but I am asking you to get some help."

"Get some help? What exactly do you mean by that?"

"Well, for starters, I think you should see a counselor."

Mamie laughed loudly. "A counselor? And how exactly is that going to help me?"

"Look, I had a chance to speak with Dorothy today. She let me know that you've had some issues with this kind of thing in the past. I think it might be helpful for you to talk to somebody about it."

"And if I don't want to?"

"Then I don't think you can stay here. We simply can't have this kind of upheaval on the island. People come here to spend their later years in a safe place where they can be happy and even build the type of family they might have never had. I won't have one person jeopardizing that."

She sat there for a long moment, thinking about what he was saying. The fact was, she was getting older, and it was extremely difficult to change at her age. Could speaking to a counselor really do anything at all?

Then the other side of her realized that if she spoke to the counselor, it meant she got to stay on Wisteria Island. It seemed like a simple enough thing to do to secure the housing that she needed.

"Fine. How do I speak to the counselor?"

"We actually have a partnership with some counselors who will do video calls with you. You don't even have to leave the island."

"You've really thought of everything here."

"We try. Also, Dorothy told me about your daughter."

"You know, I'm in trouble for gossiping, but it seems like Dorothy is doing her share of it."

"Believe it or not, I think she's a little worried about you. Even though you've hurt her deeply, she still cares what happens to you, Mamie."

"I guess I'll have to take your word for that. When I spoke to her, it certainly didn't seem like she cared much about me."

"She's just raw right now. I would venture to say that you would be too if somebody took your deepest secret and publicized it for all the world to see. Still, Dorothy was the one who asked me not to kick you off the island."

"Really?"

"She knows what it's like to start your life over at this age, and she didn't want you to have nobody. Dorothy wants you to have a second chance."

He had a point. "Wow. She's a bigger person than I would be."

"I understand that your relationship with your daughter is fractured. Here on Wisteria Island, we like to invite family to come several times a year. Is there anyone who would come visit you here?"

Mamie felt a lump forming in her throat as her stomach tightened up. "Probably not. My son lives in the Philippines and teaches English there. I don't see him very often except for the occasional video call."

"And you don't think your daughter would come?"

"My daughter doesn't even know where I am. I haven't gotten the courage to send her a letter, and I'm pretty sure she would just ignore it, anyway."

"So it seems like it's even more important for you to build a community around you here on Wisteria Island. You have to understand that in order for people to want to be there for you, they have to be able to trust you."

She knew he was right, but she didn't know how to turn off the urge to get the scoop and tell the story. It was a lot easier to have surface level friendships than it was to be vulnerable and deep.

This wasn't how she thought she would spend her older years. When she had her two kids, she assumed that as she got older, they would have kids and everybody would surround her as the grandma. She envisioned Thanksgiving and Christmas at her house, building gingerbread houses with her grandchildren and going out to see the lights.

She dreamed of sleepovers with her grandchildren, where she would read them stories as they fell asleep in her arms while she rocked them. At this point, she'd be lucky if she ever laid eyes on her new granddaughter.

Never in her wildest nightmares had she thought that she would be alone like she was. Maybe seeing a counselor would help her learn how to let people in and not feel the desire to get them before they got her.

"I'll take your offer for the counselor because I think maybe I do need that. But as for my daughter, it's probably best that she doesn't know where I am. She wouldn't care, anyway."

"I'm sure that's not true. Maybe the counselor can

help you learn how to undo the pain you've caused certain people."

"We'll see."

"Well, I'd better get back to watching the weather. We've got a lot to do before the storm rolls in day after tomorrow."

Mamie stood up and walked toward the door before turning around. "Do you think we're going to be okay here?"

He smiled, although it was a tired smile and not one of joy. "I have every reason to believe that we will all be fine."

CHAPTER 9

Danielle sat at the table, her fingers tapping against the wood veneer. Zach, seemingly oblivious to the fact that something was wrong with Bennett, continued eating his spaghetti.

"Can you please stop doing that?" He stared at her fingers.

She looked down. "Oh, sorry."

"Are you nervous about something?"

"Um, yes. My boyfriend is going to walk through that door at any minute, and he's definitely upset about something."

Zach chuckled. "You sound like a middle schooler, Danielle."

She sighed and took a bite of her garlic bread. "Okay, maybe I do, but Bennett is the best man I've ever dated. We've built something very special, and the fact that he's acting weird to me is concerning."

"You don't strike me as the type who needs a man," he said, rolling his fork around in the sauce covered noodles.

She glared at him. "I don't *need* a man. I just *want* this particular one."

"I'm sure everything is fine. Look, Bennett just lost his closest family member, and he's also worried about the possible hurricane that could blow us all out to sea. Maybe his mind is just preoccupied."

She shrugged her shoulders. "Maybe."

Just as she was calming down, Bennett walked through the door. He smiled at several residents, hugging a couple of them, before he made his way straight to her table. Maybe he was just stressed. After all, he came straight to see her, and that had to be a good sign, right?

"Hey, Bennett. Good to have you back, man," Zach said, standing up and shaking his hand. Bennett smiled slightly before sitting down at the end seat of the table.

"Good to be back."

"How are you feeling?" Danielle asked, reaching over and putting her hand on his. He looked down at their hands and pulled away, reaching into his pocket for his phone.

"Fine. Why?"

"Oh, I thought maybe you were struggling after the funeral…"

"I'm good," he said, looking down at his phone.

"Want me to get you a plate?"

"No thanks. I've got it." He stood up and walked over to the food line. Danielle looked at Zach.

"See? Something's not right."

Zach bit his lip. "Yeah, that was a little cold. I felt a literal chill."

"Not funny."

"I wasn't joking," he said under his breath.

"Line was too long. I'll get something later."

"I'm happy to share," Danielle said, sliding her plate toward him.

"It's fine, Danielle. I'll eat later. Besides, I didn't really come here for food."

"Oh? Then why are you here?"

"Well, we kind of have a huge storm heading our way, so I think the three of us should meet later tonight, watch the weather and mastermind the best course of action for riding this thing out."

"Sounds like a good idea," Zach said, wiping his mouth.

"Great. Meet at Danielle's at eight?"

Okay, apparently they were meeting at her house…

"That works for me. Danielle?"

"Yes, it works for me, too."

Bennett stood up. "Excellent. See you both then."

Without another word - and more importantly, without a hug or a kiss - Bennett walked out of the cafeteria. When she looked back at Zach, his face was full of empathy… and maybe sympathy.

"I'm so sorry, Danielle."

"For what?"

"I think you might be newly single."

Morty sat down on his sofa and stared at the TV. He had to find a new show to watch because his nights were becoming quite boring. As much as everyone thought he was the life of the party, the truth was that there just weren't enough parties.

He tried to keep busy. He tried to keep his mind off the loneliness he sometimes felt. He even tried to pretend that it didn't kill him inside that he had no one to share his life with. No significant other, but more importantly, no family.

Maybe that was why these issues with Bennett and Danielle - and Dorothy and Mamie - had hit him so hard. His early years hadn't been easy, so he was very sensitive to the idea of losing people. He'd lost his mother as a young child, and his father never understood him. He wanted Morty to play football, but Morty had been more interested in participating in theatre at school.

They didn't have those father and son moments of tossing a baseball around. They didn't go fishing or build things together. Instead, his father focused on work and starting a new family with his new wife when Morty was thirteen. Suddenly, there were all these new little kids in the house, and Morty was basically left to his own devices.

Nobody from his family came to his theatre shows, not even his sister, who was two years younger than him. She gravitated toward their father and his new wife while Morty missed his mother. She'd been his rock, and losing her had made him feel lonely in the world.

He walked over to the large buffet he had against the wall. Getting it shipped to Wisteria Island when he moved there had been quite a feat, but he loved it. It had belonged to his grandmother, then his mother, and now him. Even though he'd had to fight his sister for it years ago, he was glad it belonged to him now.

He opened the top drawer and pulled out a photo album, sitting down in one of his white upholstered Parsons chairs that sat at the dining room table. He never had guests, really, but he'd always felt having a formal dining area was important.

"Oh Momma," he said to himself, running his

thumb across her picture. He loved this one. It'd been taken when she was only twenty-five years old, but her beauty was awe-inspiring. She'd been a model in her younger years, and he could see why. Those high cheekbones. That porcelain skin. Those crystal clear blue eyes, although everything was black and white in photos from that long ago.

He rarely took out his photo album because it made him sad to look through it, but sometimes he just needed to feel those feelings. His life hadn't gone the way he'd intended, but if there was anything Morty knew how to do, it was make the best of what he had. He would not let people get to him, and if they did, he would not let them see him sweat.

Morty turned a few of the pages, smiling as he looked at photos of himself back in the sixties and seventies. Some of the outfits he wore made him cringe now, but it was the style back then. Oh, what he wouldn't give for just one day. Just one day to go back and live in that time when he was young and full of hope and plans for the future. Just one day to relive old places, old friends and a youthful body.

Things creaked when he got up now. In the morning, he felt like he needed to oil his joints before he could walk. Even though he was pretty spry compared to many, he still felt like his body was getting older, no matter what he did. Or maybe today he was just in a funk.

Thankfully, he always snapped out of funks pretty fast. No sense in dwelling on the negative, as his mother used to say. "Get up and get on with it", she'd tell him when he was upset over how people treated him at school. Never known as normal or typical, Morty didn't have many close friends until he got to college. He found people more accepting of his eccentricities there.

Being short - barely five feet tall - didn't do him any favors either. Nobody ever picked him for team sports, and he certainly had his share of terrible nicknames over the years. Peewee. The little leprechaun. Stumpy. Scooter. Pipsqueak. And a few others he tried to never think about.

So when he thought about the upcoming family visit, he felt his stomach tighten up all over again. He hated standing out by the dock, waiting for someone to show up. He hated spending holidays without any family, and not even a Christmas card. But he stood by that dock and kept a smile on his face because his chosen family - his Wisteria Island community - needed him there. He took his support of them very seriously.

Suddenly, he was startled out of his trip down memory lane by the sound of his cell phone ringing. He so very rarely got calls, but he assumed it was Bennett wanting to chat about the oncoming storm preparations. He relied on Morty to gather the troops and get people to do what they were supposed to.

He walked over and picked up his phone, which had been charging on the end table by the sofa. The number wasn't one he recognized. "Hello?"

"Oh, hi. Um, is this Morty?"

The voice on the other end was a young woman, possibly in her late teens or maybe early twenties. Either that or whoever it was just had a younger sounding voice. "Yes, this is Morty. Who's this?"

"My name is Lacey, and I'm your great niece."

His breath caught in his chest. He had a great niece? How had he not known that? "Wait, so you're Darla's daughter then?"

Morty's sister was Alice, but she'd died about fourteen years previously. Her daughter was Darla, and Morty had never really had a relationship with her other than seeing her in passing at family funerals. He and Alice had never had a close relationship, so he certainly didn't get to be in Darla's life, and she hadn't reached out once she was an adult. To say this call was a surprise would be an understatement.

"Yes, my mom is Darla."

"Honey, how old are you?"

"I just turned eighteen."

"Wow. I didn't even know you existed, but it's nice to meet you."

"It's nice to meet you, too. Can I call you Uncle Morty? I don't have an uncle."

He smiled. "Of course you can. I'm really surprised to hear from you, Lacey. I didn't think my family talked about me much."

She cleared her throat. "Well, they don't very much, but I found some old pictures and asked my mom."

"Oh? And what did she say?"

"Not too much."

"Darlin', it's okay to tell me the truth."

She took in a deep breath and he could hear her shakily let it back out. "They said you didn't fit into the family and that you were… weird."

He let out a loud laugh. "Well, that's the truth! And I'm proud of it!"

She giggled, the sound of relief in her voice. "That's why I wanted to find you."

"Why's that?"

"Because I'm weird too, and I'd like to know more about you, Uncle Morty."

His eyes welled with tears. "You're weird too, huh?"

"Yes, sir. Mom wants me to go to college to be a lawyer, but I want to be a Reiki master and energy healer."

Morty paused for a moment, unsure of what to say, since he had no clue what either of those phrases meant. He just knew he wanted this lifeline, this family connection.

"That's wonderful, dear. Always follow your heart. Nobody else has to walk in your shoes."

"Thank you! I'm so glad to hear at least one adult tell me it's okay to follow my passion. Do you think I could visit you soon?"

Morty put his hand over his heart. "I would absolutely love that."

"Great! Can you text me and let me know how to visit?"

Morty laughed. "Honey, I don't have a clue how to text, but I can send email. Is that okay?"

Lacey giggled. "Of course. My email is…"

After writing down her email address and saying their goodbyes, Morty ended the call and fell onto the sofa. Laying on his back, he grinned like a Cheshire Cat as he stared up at the ceiling. A great-niece. A member of his family who wanted to know him. Miracles happened after all.

"Hey," Danielle said as she opened the door for Bennett. He stood there, hands in the pockets of his khaki shorts.

"Hey. Can I come in?"

"Of course," she said, opening the door wider and

stepping back. Why did their relationship suddenly feel so weird? Did they even have a relationship anymore?

"Where's Zach?"

"He's coming. Estelle Friedman hurt her elbow, so he had to meet her at the clinic after dinner. Tennis injury, from what I understand. Cup of coffee?"

"Sure."

He followed her into the kitchen and sat at the breakfast bar. The awkwardness between them was thick, and she didn't really know what to say. "Black, right?"

"Yep."

She slid the cup of coffee over to him and stood across the counter from him. "How are you doing?"

"Fine. And you?"

"Fine," she said softly. "Listen, are you mad at me?"

He looked down at his coffee before answering. "No. Why would you ask?"

"Because things seem to have changed between us since you got back. Did I do something wrong?"

"I have no idea. Did you?"

She was taken aback. "Not that I know of."

"Then everything is fine, right?" He looked at her for a moment before returning to looking at his coffee again.

"Right."

"Sorry I'm late," Zach said, walking through the front door quickly.

"I guess he doesn't have to knock," Bennett mumbled under his breath. Danielle heard it, but chose not to say anything.

Zach walked into the kitchen and sat down at the table. "So, what are we talking about?"

"Nothing much so far," Danielle said.

Bennett reached down into his bag and pulled out his laptop, opening it without saying a word. "Okay, here's what the weather is looking like so far. Tomorrow morning, the strong winds are going to start. I've got Darryl, Jeremy, and Eddie working on sandbags right now. Every building has hurricane shutters, so we'll get everything closed up well before the winds start."

"Are they still predicting that it'll hit us head on?" Zach asked.

"No. It's going to turn a little eastward, so we'll get a decent hit, but not as bad as we originally worried."

Danielle put her hand on her heart. "Oh, thank goodness. Zach and I did everything we could while you were gone."

"I'm sure you did," Bennett said, again under his breath. What was his deal?

"Excuse me?"

He looked at her. "I'm sure the two of you worked together to get things done."

She paused for a moment. "We definitely did. We hauled a lot of residents off this island. We found places for them to stay. We worked our tails off to do what we could. I can't tell if you're being sarcastic or what, but you should know we did everything we could possibly do to protect the residents of this island." She was getting angry now, and she didn't even know why.

"I think tension is high right now…" Zach said, trying to calm things down.

"You're right, Zach. Tensions are definitely high right now. We have a dangerous storm heading our way, and we need to focus." Even as Bennett spoke, he looked at Danielle. There was a mixture of anger and hurt in his eyes, and she was completely confused.

"What can I do?" Zach asked, obviously eager to get the heck out of there.

Bennett turned and looked at him. "Can you go help Darryl and the other guys with the sandbags? They definitely need more help, and you're a young, strapping guy, right?"

Zach furrowed his eyebrows. "I suppose I am…"

"I mean, unless that work is beneath a fancy doctor like yourself?"

"Of course not."

"Great."

Zach slowly turned and walked out the front door, looking back at Danielle one last time, confusion written all over his face.

"What was that about?"

Bennett stood up and started packing his laptop into his bag. "What?"

She stood to face him. "You know what? You've been acting strange ever since you got back. I've tried so hard to be understanding, but you're making it more and more difficult to have compassion for you."

"Is that what you've had for me, Danielle? Compassion?"

Her jaw clenched. "Why do I feel like we're speaking different languages lately?"

Bennett walked across the kitchen and put his hands on the breakfast bar, leaning into it. "Do you want to tell me something?"

She crossed her arms and looked at him. "I don't know what you're talking about."

He sighed. "Look, if you're interested in Zach, just tell me. Your job isn't in jeopardy. I'm not that kind of man or boss."

Her eyes widened. "What?"

"I get it. He's younger than me. He's got those perfect muscles and thicker hair. He's a doctor…"

"Are you interested in dating him, then?"

He looked at her. "You think this is funny?"

"No. I think this is *ridiculous*."

"I'm trying to give you an out, Danielle."

She walked closer and stood on the other side of the counter. "Bennett, I've never been more confused in my life. Why are you trying to get me to be with Zach?"

"I saw you."

"Saw me what?"

"I saw you dancing."

Danielle paused for a moment before bursting into laughter. "Oh, my gosh! Seriously?"

"I came to see you, and when you didn't answer the door, I walked around back."

"And you spied on us?"

He pushed himself off the counter and paced a couple of times back and forth. "Spied on you? Am I not allowed to come to my girlfriend's house?"

"Of course you are! But I expect you to speak and not hide in the bushes like a stalker!"

"Morty said…"

She rolled her eyes. "I love Morty, but he's been making stories up in his head and nothing I say to him will stop him from worrying that we're going to break up."

"You were dancing the tango, Danielle."

She smiled. "Zach met a woman on the mainland, and she wants their first date to be at a ballroom dancing club. I mentioned that I took lessons as a kid, so I was teaching him some basic dances for his date, Bennett. As a friend. Nothing else."

He stood there for a moment, taking in her words. "You were teaching him?"

"Yes."

"But Morty said you were getting close while I was gone."

"He's my co-worker. We do the same work. We treat the same patients. You told me to make him feel welcome."

He put his hands over his face. "I feel like the world's biggest fool."

"You should."

She turned around and walked into the living room, sitting down on the sofa. Bennett followed and sat on the coffee table across from her. "I'm so sorry."

"Okay." She really was upset that he didn't trust her, and that he'd acted so juvenile about all of it. It made her uncomfortable.

"Can you forgive me?"

"I forgive you, Bennett. But I'm not sure what this says about our relationship right now."

"What?"

"You didn't trust me. You didn't talk to me. You acted like a child. You automatically assumed that I would cheat and lie. Those aren't good things for a relationship."

"I guess I just got jealous and worried."

"Look, I just got out of a dysfunctional relationship right before I came here. I don't need another one."

"Danielle, what are you saying?"

"I'm saying maybe we need to take a break."

His face fell, and he reached over to take her hands. "Please don't say that. I trust you. I just had a temporary moment of bad self-esteem. Zach is a good-looking guy, and he's a doctor."

"So what? You're a gazillionaire. What does being a doctor have to do with anything?"

"He understands you."

"I thought you did, too. Can you just go?"

"Danielle..."

"Bennett, please go. I need some time to think."

He sucked in a deep breath and blew it out before standing up. He picked up his bag and walked toward the door, turning back toward her one more time. "I love you."

"I love you too, but as the cliche says, sometimes love just isn't enough."

CHAPTER 10

MAMIE SAT IN FRONT OF HER COMPUTER, THE blinking cursor flashing like a neon sign. This time, she wasn't trying to think up a story. She was trying to gather her courage to email her daughter.

Naomi at the front office had helped her secure an appointment with the counselor to do a virtual session after the storm passed. Hopefully, the internet would be back up by the time of her appointment.

Before her appointment, Mamie had decided she wanted to reach out to her daughter. She wanted to prove to the therapist how her daughter wanted nothing to do with her. Deep down, she wanted closure - good or bad. Likely bad.

Her hands dangled over the keyboard like a puppet with its arms frozen in air. Why couldn't she do this? How did she even start? What words would pierce through the internet and touch her daughter's steel-encased heart?

She took in a few deep breaths and allowed her fingers to type.

Dear Connie,

I know you'll probably be surprised to hear from me, but maybe not. It's been a long time, and you might just delete this email, but please finish reading it first. It took all my strength to write it.

I've made some big mistakes in my life, and I recently made another one. At my age, I should be better than this. Regret is my constant companion, but I'm also human. There must be some part of me that chooses to sabotage my life repeatedly.

I'm sorry for what I did to you. It was wrong, and I've regretted it every day since. My love for you will never change, and I want you to know that I'm here if you ever want to reach out. I'll tell you I'm sorry every day for the rest of my life if that's what it takes.

Being alone at my age isn't what I had planned, but it's what I caused. I know that. You shouldn't feel sorry for me, not that you do. I put myself in this position. But, it doesn't mean I don't ache to have my kids in my life. Your brother is a world away, but I hear from him every now and again. I'm thankful for that. I long for my daughter, though.

I now live in a place called Wisteria Island, just off the

South Carolina coast. It's a retirement community, and it's lovely. I made a new friend, but then I betrayed her trust and now I'm alone again. So, I'm doing something I never thought I'd do - I'm going to therapy. Can you believe it?

They say you can't teach an old dog new tricks, but I hope this old dog can learn how to live a different life and be a different person. I want to be better for you, for your brother and for myself.

Well, a hurricane is heading this way, so we're battening down the hatches and riding it out. I guess I wanted to just say how much I love you, just in case we get swept out to sea or something. I'm sure it'll be fine, though. It's hard to kill a tough old bird like me.

I love you, Connie. And even if I never get to hug you again, I will always hold you in my heart.

Love,

Mom

Danielle awoke with a jolt, the sound of high winds whipping around her cottage. She jumped out of bed and looked out the window, surprised to see how quickly the weather had turned. She got dressed, grabbed the bag she'd packed, and headed out the door. Thankfully, the gymnasium, where everyone was to gather, was just a few doors down. Still, the walk was hard. If this was just the precursor to the storm, they might be in for a rough time.

She hadn't slept well at all last night, partly over worrying about the storm but mostly because of her conversation with Bennett. She was still so angry at him for not trusting her and thinking she'd actually cheat on him. After all, they were still in that honeymoon phase. Well, they had been anyway. Now she had no idea where their relationship was going.

"You okay?" Zach called as he met her on the sidewalk in front of the gym.

"Yeah. It got bad out here pretty quickly, though."

"Come on, let's get inside," he yelled over the winds.

They walked into the gym to find many residents already sitting around the tables, some eating breakfast and others playing cards. Morty was asleep with his head on the table. She didn't see Bennett yet, and part of her worried about him getting there since his cottage was on the other side of the island.

She saw Eddie and Jeremy ushering more residents into the building. She knew their job was to get as many residents into the building as possible, going door to door to make sure they knew the storm had begun. They didn't want to leave anyone in their cottage.

"Is there anything we can do to help?" Zach asked Eddie.

"I think we've pretty much gotten everyone over here. Some of them gave me quite a time. They didn't want to leave their homes, but it's not safe for them to stay, even with the hurricane shutters. I spoke to Bennett this morning, and he said the storm turned again, so we might get more of a hit than we thought."

"Well, it's too late to get off the island, so we're going to have to hunker down here," Danielle said, stating the obvious.

"How is everybody?" Bennett said, seeming to appear from nowhere. He, too, looked tired and like he hadn't slept. There were bags under his eyes, and his hair was a mess from the wind outside.

"I think we've got everybody. Sand bags all stacked up. Hurricane shutters on every building. Golf carts parked in the garage with doors closed."

"And the boat?"

"Tied down as tight as we could get it," Jeremy said.

"Have we called to check on our residents on the mainland?"

"I called all of them last night, and everyone is doing well," Zach said.

"Good. We've done the best we can under the circumstances. Can you guys go mingle with the residents a bit and make sure everybody got something for breakfast?" Zach, Eddie and Jeremy all nodded and went their separate ways, leaving Danielle alone with Bennett.

"I'd better go help them," she said. Bennett grabbed her arm.

"Danielle, about last night…"

She held up her hand. "Bennett, now is not the time. We're kind of in a high-stress situation here. My focus is on our residents."

He sighed. "You're right. I'm sorry. It's just that I hate this feeling between us, and I didn't sleep."

"I need to go check on Morty."

He released his grip on her arm. "Okay."

As Danielle walked away from him, all she wanted to do was turn back and run straight into his arms. She was scared.

Scared of the storm. Scared of them breaking up. Scared that she was going to push this too far and lose the love of her life.

Dorothy stared down at her fingernails. "The pink or the red?"

Morty leaned over the table slightly. "Go with the red. Always go with the red."

She chuckled and opened the bottle of nail polish. "Should we feel bad that she's sitting over there alone? She looks like a stray dog."

Morty turned his head slightly so as not to let Mamie see him looking at her. "She made her bed."

"We're sitting here in the middle of a hurricane, or maybe just a really bad tropical storm. Either way, perhaps we shouldn't let her sit over there alone."

"Dorothy, I can't believe you would want to have anything to do with her. I mean, after what she did to you? I don't know that I'd ever speak to her again."

"I know, I know. She totally screwed up. She's probably a horrible person. But I still feel bad watching her sit over there by herself. This is pretty stressful, this whole storm."

He shrugged his shoulders. "I don't know. It isn't really bothering me much. I mean, it's loud out there, but so far the roof hasn't blown off."

"I don't think the full storm is even here yet. I overheard Bennett say it would be a few more hours before it would actually hit the island. So we're stuck in here for a long time."

"How boring. I hate being stuck inside."

"You know, I talked to a TV station last night."

Morty looked up and stared at her. "You did what?"

"Yeah, Naomi told me that this big station in California called, and I called them back. I was tired of hiding."

"I thought you didn't want your dirty laundry out there."

"To be fair, it wasn't my dirty laundry. I was the victim."

"I know. You're right. Well, how did it go? What did they say?"

"It actually went really well. Not as bad as I thought it would. They wanted to know the story from my perspective, and I told it to them. It actually made me feel like I had a big weight off my shoulders. I didn't realize I'd been carrying that around."

"I wish I could've seen it. Maybe we could pull it up on the Internet?"

She waved her hand. "Oh, I don't know. You know, I don't have a clue how any of that stuff works."

He turned his head again and noticed the closed laptop sitting next to Mamie. She was sitting at a table alone, her hands resting in front of her. She didn't even have much of a look on her face. She just looked distant. It had to be hard for her to sit in a room full of people who were all mad at her. Plus, she was going to be stuck there for hours.

"Maybe we could borrow Mamie's computer."

Dorothy looked up. "Are you serious? The very same computer she used to write the story in the first place?"

"Well, she owes you at least that."

Dorothy sat there and thought for a moment. "Okay, fine. But I'm not asking her."

Morty stood up and walked toward Mamie. At first, she looked very concerned when she saw him coming, but her face eased up once he was in front of her.

"Hi, Mamie."

She cleared her throat. "Oh, hi."

"Listen, Dorothy and I were wondering if we could borrow your computer for a few minutes?"

She looked at him for a long moment, like she was trying to decide whether to say yes or no, worried about making people even madder at her.

"I suppose so…"

She slid it closer to Morty and then sighed, looking off to her side. "Ugh. Mamie, do you want to sit with us?"

Shocked, she looked back at him. "Really?"

"Well, it appears we might all perish in a hurricane, so we might as well let you sit with us. More points when we meet God."

Mamie stifled a smile. "Thanks."

She stood up and followed him back to the table, stopping only to decide whether to sit beside Dorothy or Morty. She chose Morty, although he didn't know why. He wasn't any more on her side than Dorothy was.

"Now, how do you use this thing?" Morty said, opening it up and putting on his reading glasses. He kept them in his shirt pocket even though he hated the darn things. They made him feel like an old man.

"You just click that button there, and it'll take you to the internet," she said, leaning toward him. "What exactly are we looking for?"

Morty looked at Dorothy. "We have to tell her so she can help us find it."

Dorothy rolled her eyes and waved one of her newly painted hands toward him. "Fine. I did an interview with a TV station last night. It was one of those phone video interview things. Morty wanted to see it."

Mamie looked stunned. "You mean because of my..."

"Your unauthorized gossip story? Yes, that one," Dorothy said, her voice as snooty as Morty had ever heard it.

"I just thought you didn't want to be contacted about it..."

"I didn't, but someone took that choice away from me."

"I'm so sorry, Dorothy."

"Let's not rehash it again. Just show Morty how to find it."

Mamie scooted toward him and turned the computer to face him. "We should be able to do a news search here... Type in your name... Here it is!"

Morty took the computer back and clicked on the link. "Ready?"

"As I'll ever be," Dorothy said, dryly. They gathered around the laptop and watched the story, none of them saying anything. When it was over, Morty closed the laptop.

"Wow, Dorothy. That was quite a story."

"You told it so eloquently, too. So much better than I did."

Dorothy looked at her like she wanted to say something mean, but she refrained. "Thank you."

"How do you feel about it now?" Morty asked.

She thought for a moment. "I actually feel relieved. I never wanted to tell the story, and it's not the way I would've done it if I had wanted to tell it, but I'm glad it's done."

Mamie sat in silence, obviously not wanting to take any credit for putting it out there. Morty thought that was a wise decision on her part.

"I want you to know I talked to Bennett, and he told me I have to get counseling if I want to continue living here." She blurted it out like she'd been holding it in for days.

"Oh? And how do you feel about that?" Dorothy asked, not really looking at her.

"At first, I thought it was ridiculous, but I've had some time to think. I really believe it's going to help me learn to trust people and strengthen relation-ships. At least I hope so."

"I hope so too," Dorothy said.

"And thank you for asking Bennett not to kick me off the island. You didn't have to do that."

"You did that?" Morty said, shocked.

Dorothy nodded. "I did do that. My mother always taught me that two wrongs don't make a right. Being spiteful and getting Mamie kicked out of her new home wouldn't have made me feel any better."

"You're a better person than I am," Morty muttered.

"I also want you to know I emailed my daughter last night. I haven't heard back from her, but I hope to."

"Glad to hear it, Mamie. As mad as I've been, I really do wish good things for you. I know what it's like to be misunderstood and to have a hard time making friends."

Morty couldn't believe what he was hearing. Dorothy really had changed a lot since coming to the island. She was gentler and kinder than her former self.

"Thank you, Dorothy. And I hope one day we can try to be friends again."

Dorothy laughed. "Don't push it, Mamie. For

now, maybe we can coexist in groups. But I won't be telling you any more secrets."

"Smart cookie, you are, Dorothy," Mamie said, chuckling.

"How's the radar looking?" Zach asked, walking up behind Danielle. He sat down next to her.

"Bad," she said, matter-of-factly. Thankfully, Zach had remembered to bring his laptop, although the Wi-Fi signal was going in and out, and she assumed it would be gone completely within the next couple of hours.

If she was honest, she was nervous about being on an island in the middle of a hurricane. Even though they weren't getting a direct hit, it was close enough to make her anxious. And she wasn't an anxious person. She was tough as steel when she needed to be, like when she had to give families bad news in the ICU. But right now, she kind of wanted to curl up in the fetal position.

"Yeah, that looks pretty rough. I've never been in a storm like this before."

"Neither have I." She sighed and closed the computer.

"You okay?"

She looked up and noticed Bennett in the corner

of the gym, talking to Eddie. "Not really. Bennett and I broke up. I think."

"You think?"

"Turns out, he saw us dancing the other night and got the wrong idea."

Zach's eyes widened. "What? How did he see us?"

"He came to my house, walked around back and saw us."

"And he didn't say anything?"

"My point exactly. He didn't speak, assumed the worst, and then acted like a very rich toddler for a few days. I can't handle someone not trusting me."

"So you broke up with him?"

"I said I needed a break."

Zach laughed. "What does that mean?"

"I'm not exactly sure."

"Listen, I don't want to butt my nose in where it doesn't belong, but from what you've said, you adore Bennett."

"I really do."

"Then maybe take some of this time we have to sit down and talk to him?"

"I don't think I'm ready for that."

He chuckled. "Do you really mean you want to make him squirm for a while?"

She looked at him. "Why would you say that?"

Zach held up his hands. "At the risk of sounding

sexist or chauvinistic or whatever, sometimes women seem to enjoy making us suffer for a bit."

She stifled a smile. "Sometimes you deserve it."

"Agreed, but if this is the relationship you want long-term, one of you needs to act like an adult."

She laid her head on the table. "I hate being stuck in this gym. It's making me stir crazy."

"I know. I feel the same way."

She sat back up and looked at Bennett, who was now talking to Gladys. There was no telling what she was talking about. Gladys, although medicated and doing well, still had a vivid imagination.

CHAPTER 11

"So, what do you think?" Gladys asked, her eyes lit up with excitement.

"Bungee jumping?"

"Yes! I saw a whole bit about it on the news. You get up on this high bridge, they tie your feet up with some kind of springy rope and away you go!" She held her hands in the air and screamed, and several residents turned around. Once they realized it was just Gladys being Gladys, they went back to playing cards and crocheting hats.

"Gladys, I love your zest for life, but do you really think a bunch of seniors should be jumping off of bridges?" Bennett appreciated her enthusiasm, but he really wasn't up for her crazy ideas today.

"Oh, why not? I get tired of bingo and square dancing. I need a little excitement in my life."

"Bennett, do you have a second?"

"Sure, Eddie. I'll check back with you later, Gladys, okay?" She nodded and smiled, looking back down at her crossword puzzle before he even left the table.

"What's up?"

"We're definitely getting some damage out there. I was able to access a couple of the cameras before they went out, and we've lost some parts of the cafe's roof. Flooding has also started near the dock."

"Dang it. I was hoping we'd get out of this unscathed. What's the radar showing?"

"We keep losing Wi-Fi, and our cell signals aren't picking up. I was last able to check it about fifteen minutes ago. Looks like the eye hit further north, so we're getting some of the stronger bands. If we can make it through the night, we should be fine by morning."

Bennett hated all of this. Of course, hurricanes had been part of his thinking when he bought an island and put a bunch of retirees on it, but he thought he'd prepared for it. Now he was wondering if he'd been way less prepared than he thought.

"The most important thing is everyone's safety. We can replace material things. See if you can check any of the other cameras."

Eddie nodded and walked off quickly as Bennett leaned against the wall and rubbed the space between his eyes. That night of no sleep was really catching up with him. When he opened his eyes, Zach was standing in front of him.

"I feel like we need to have a conversation."

Bennett sighed. "Right now?"

"I think so."

Bennett turned to see Danielle sitting with her back to them at a table with Mr. Mathis and Mrs. Calhoun. The two of them had started dating, and Danielle enjoyed hearing about their dates.

"Okay, what is it?"

"I want you to know that I have no interest in Danielle. We are co-workers and very new friends, but nothing else."

"I know. I overreacted to what I saw, and I should've asked Danielle what was going on. I was just exhausted after watching my great aunt die, and all that travel…"

"I get it. When I lost my dad, I wasn't myself either. Everything put me on edge, and I was angry for a long time."

"I wish Danielle could understand."

"I think she will, in time. She loves you."

"She told you that?"

"Several times," Zach said, smiling.

"Then why is she punishing me?"

"Have you ever dated a woman?"

Bennett laughed. "Right."

"Just don't give up on her. Apparently, you trusting her is very important."

"I see that now. And I'm sorry for thinking that you'd do something like that either…"

Zach put up his hand. "Look, you barely know me. I can see how you might think what you did. But, again, I assure you I respect your relationship with Danielle, and my thoughts of her are as a co-worker and nothing else. Plus, I have a date with a very nice woman I met on the mainland."

Bennett chuckled. "You mean the dancing date?"

"Yes, the dancing date. I'll probably break one of her toes."

"Well, at least you can handle her medical care for free!"

"I can't believe we lost internet completely," Morty said, staring at Mamie's computer. He'd spent the last two hours playing a word game, and now he was addicted and probably needed a twelve-step program.

"The battery's getting low anyway," Mamie said, sliding the computer back toward her. "I forgot my charger back at the cottage."

"Rookie mistake," Morty said.

"You took up so much time, I never got to check

my email," she said, clicking over to her inbox. Emails had downloaded while everything was online, but she couldn't pull anything up other than subject lines since the internet was down now. "Oh, my goodness!"

"What?" Dorothy asked.

"My daughter responded."

"She did?"

Mamie clicked on the email over and over, but to no avail. "I can't see what she said. It just shows that she responded. Oh my gosh, my stomach is in knots!"

"You just need to think good thoughts. Maybe it's a lovely email," Dorothy said. Mamie was happy that they were getting along because she needed friends right now. She was sure the email was hateful, or at least telling her to bug off and leave her alone.

"I can't handle this stress. Somebody distract me," Mamie said, shutting the laptop.

"The last time I tried to distract you, I ended up on the TV news."

"Very funny."

"No, very true," Dorothy said, pursing her lips.

"Morty? You got anything?"

"My great-niece, who I didn't know existed, called me yesterday out of the blue and wants to meet me. She wants to come visit and get to know me."

"What? And you didn't tell me?" Dorothy shrieked. "That's fabulous, right?"

"I sure hope so. My little heart can't take getting jilted by my family again. She seemed so nice, though. Her name is Lacey, and she's eighteen years old."

"That's just wonderful, Morty," Mamie said.

"She's the oddball of her family too, so I think she feels like I'll understand her. She wants to be some kind of energy healer and rake people?"

Mamie pondered for a moment. "Are you sure she didn't say Reiki?"

"Yes, that's it! What on earth does that even mean? She rakes people's backs or something?"

Mamie laughed. "Only because I lived in California for a time, do I even know what that is. It's a type of Japanese energy healing. They use their hands and a power they've been given by another Reiki healer."

"Sounds like a bunch of new age hogwash to me," Dorothy said, rolling her eyes.

"Well, I don't know what to think about it, but I'm going to support her no matter what. She's my family, and I'm just tickled pink to get to meet her."

Dorothy reached over and squeezed his hand. "I know you are, Morty. And you deserve this. I'm so thrilled for you."

The night wore on, the seemingly endless sound of wind whipping around the building. Danielle had never been so tired in her life, and that included her long shifts in the ICU. Managing the needs of most of her residents in one room while the edges of a hurricane battered their beloved island was a lot to handle. Her nerves were frazzled, and she wanted to go bury her head in Bennett's warm chest. But she couldn't. Because she stupidly said she wanted a break.

She didn't want a break.

She might have a breakdown instead.

If there was one thing she'd learned as the daughter of two doctors, it was that she could never let anyone see when she was wrong. Being right - being trustworthy in the eyes of her patients - was the most important thing. That, unfortunately, translated over to her relationships as well.

There was no way she could go tell Bennett that she'd made a mistake with this whole "taking a break" thing, and that she forgave him. She'd look ridiculous, as if she didn't already feel that way.

She leaned her back against the concrete wall of the gym and surveyed the scene. It was after one in the morning now, and all the residents were sacked out. Cots had been set up all across the gym, and the sound of snores and wind gusts were all she could hear. So far, the gym had fared well, but none of them had a clue what it looked like outside. Internet access had been down for hours, and the cameras were non-functional at this point.

"Why don't you get some sleep? There's an empty cot over next to Morty," Zach said as he walked up with a Styrofoam cup full of coffee.

"I'm still too wired. I'm fine here. Have you seen Bennett?"

"He's asleep over next to Gladys. She finally stopped talking long enough for him to doze off."

So Bennett could sleep and she couldn't. Maybe he wasn't worried about their relationship after all. Or maybe she was just a little too punchy after being awake for so long.

"Why aren't you sleeping?"

"I'm not tired either. Too much coffee, I think." He pulled up a chair and sat next to her, his back against the cold wall. "What do you think this place will look like come morning?"

She shrugged her shoulders. "I don't know, but I'm pretty afraid to find out."

"Me too. I haven't been here long, but I like it here."

"I'm sure we'll be fine. This community is strong, and we'll repair the damage and move on."

"I sometimes wonder why Bennett created this

place. I mean, the man has a lot of money. He could go anywhere and do anything. Why does he choose to spend his life here with a bunch of older people?"

"He had a rough childhood, but he had a grandmother he adored. He wished she got a better ending to her life than a dingy nursing home, so Wisteria Island was born from that. He's a good man, and he followed through to honor her memory."

"But he could've created this place, had someone else run it and move to, I don't know, the south of France. Why stay here?"

She'd often thought about that herself. Was he in witness protection? Was he hiding from a long lost, crazy girlfriend? Or maybe her imagination was getting away from her due to lack of sleep.

"You're asking me hard questions, and my brain is fried," she said, her eyes getting heavier.

"Danielle, go get some sleep. I'll watch everybody. I promise."

She considered arguing with him, but he was right. She was tired, and keeping herself awake was just going to make everything harder in the morning.

"Okay. But you wake me up if you need anything."

He smiled and nodded. "Yes, ma'am."

As she walked to her cot near Morty - who snored like a freight train and obviously needed to be checked for sleep apnea - she looked over at Bennett. He seemed to be peacefully sleeping, and she had to wonder if maybe he was okay with this break they were taking. Maybe she loved him more than he loved her.

Morning came early for Bennett. He'd listened to the sound of snoring seniors for hours, along with the sound of the wind knocking things around outside. It had kind of been like sleeping at a hospital, where constant interruptions from nurses keep you up all night. He'd never been great about sleeping anywhere other than his own bed, but sleeping on a cot in the middle of a drafty gymnasium with dozens of other people was a new low.

"Good morning!" He turned his head to see Gladys already sitting up, a smile on her face. She was eating a blueberry muffin and had apparently been watching Bennett sleep. His eyes were still a bit blurry, so he rubbed them and slowly sat up.

"Good morning, Gladys. How'd you sleep?"

"I always sleep great. My secret is earplugs and a nice shot of whiskey."

"Gladys, you know you shouldn't be drinking with your medications."

She waved her hand. "Oh, hogwash! I think it makes my medicines work even better."

He decided not to push it and talk to Danielle or Zach about it later. "Where'd you get that muffin?"

"Eddie put them out on that table over there." She pointed across the gym, and as Bennett's eyes scanned the room, he noticed Danielle just waking up. She was sitting up, stretching her arms high above her head.

"Thanks." He stood up and slipped his sneakers back on before heading toward the table. He needed some food before they opened the doors to survey the damage that had been caused overnight.

"Morning, boss," Eddie said as Bennett approached.

"Good morning. Has anyone looked outside yet?"

"No, sir. We were waiting for you. Sun hasn't finished coming up anyway, I don't think."

"Good. Gives me time to scarf down a couple of muffins and some coffee. It's going to be a long day."

"I do believe you're right."

"Good morning, everyone," Danielle said, being careful to not make eye contact. This was killing him. He wanted to reach out and hug her. He would've loved to have her curled up beside him in his cot while they rode out the storm together. Instead, they were on a "break". What did that even mean?

"Good morning," he said softly, hoping she'd look at him. Instead, she bit into a muffin and walked away. Eddie eyed him carefully.

"Trouble in paradise?"

"Nothing feels like paradise right now, my friend. Well, except maybe this muffin. Where'd we get these?"

"Jeremy picked them up at a bakery in Seagrove."

"Very good. Okay, I guess we should slip out the side entrance and see what it looks like out there?"

"Just the two of us?"

"I think so, at least for now. I don't want to wake the rest of them up until we know more."

Eddie and Bennett made their way to the side door and cracked it open, both of them peeking outside like a monster was going to attack at any moment.

"Wow," Eddie said as his eyes adjusted to the morning light peeking over the horizon. The sky was pink and orange, beautiful as ever, like it was unaware of the violent storm that had just passed through the area.

"Oh my goodness," Bennett said, following him out the door. His eyes were overwhelmed by the amount of damage he saw in front of him. Somewhere, in the optimistic part of his brain, he'd hoped only a few limbs would be down in the street.

"Looks like we have a lot of roofing that needs to

be done," Eddie said, doing a full turn and looking up.

"Yes, we do. The cafe is a mess, but the clinic looks pretty good. At least that's a blessing."

They continued walking, and then Eddie retrieved one of the golf carts from the garage. He pulled in front of the gym to pick up Bennett.

"I'd like to ride along."

Bennett turned to see Danielle standing behind him, her arms crossed and hugging her body.

"Of course."

They each climbed into the golf cart and Eddie began slowly driving down the streets. At least this time he couldn't go very fast because of all the debris on the roads.

"We have so much cleanup to do," Bennett said.

"The cottages look like they fared pretty well, aside from some shingles that will need replacing."

"Not all of them," Danielle said, pointing in the opposite direction. There was a line of cottages, each with part of their roof sheared off.

"Dear God," Bennett said, putting his hand over his mouth.

"The residents will have to double up while we get repairs done," Bennett said. "No way they can stay here."

"Let's check your house out while we're down this way, Bennett," Eddie said. He turned the corner and pulled in front of Bennett's house. They all stepped out and started walking around.

"Everything looks pretty good," Bennett said, carefully looking up and down. "Just need to move some debris out of the yard, but otherwise I came out pretty unscathed, it seems."

"You were definitely lucky, my friend," Eddie said, slapping him on the back as they climbed into the golf cart again.

They continued going up and down streets, Bennett making notes on his phone about everything that needed to be done. The cafe had taken a pretty major hit, as had a whole street of cottages. There were trees down and lots of debris. Some houses had flooding that would need to be attended to quickly. Others looked no worse for the wear.

"Let's check Danielle's cottage," Bennett said as they headed to the other end of the island. As they pulled in front of it, they all sat in silence for a long moment.

"Oh no," Bennett said. Her cottage was all but destroyed. The whole roof was gone, the porch was hanging on by a thread and ironically, the deck out back was still standing like a stage. The walls were still standing, but everything inside the cottage was waterlogged.

"Dani, I'm so sorry…" Eddie said, squeezing her

shoulder as she walked around the side of the golf cart. "Seems your place took a direct hit."

They waited for her to make a sound, to say anything, but she just stared at her home with a blank look on her face. Bennett was getting a little worried.

"Danielle?"

She stayed silent for a moment. "Yeah?"

"Are you okay?"

Danielle started laughing, but not the kind of laugh you hear when someone has told a funny joke. This was more like the laugh of a person who is losing their sanity.

"Am I okay? Well, let's see… A hurricane just destroyed my home with all of my possessions in it. Would you be fine with that?"

"No. I'm sorry," Bennett said. Sensing this was a private moment, Eddie walked further away and surveyed the damage closer. Bennett stood beside the cart. "Danielle, what can I do or say?"

"I feel like this is a sign or something."

"A sign?"

"Well, we broke up… or something… and now my house blew away. Maybe I'm not meant to be here."

"You know that's not true. And I don't accept that being on a break means we broke up."

She sighed and stood up, walking closer to the cottage. "Do you think it's safe to go inside?"

"I don't know. Maybe Darryl should go inside first."

"Darryl is on the mainland with his family," Eddie said, walking back toward them. "We might be able to get him back over here tomorrow, depending on the waves and any damage on the mainland. Phones and Wi-Fi still ain't working."

"I lost everything."

"Now, you don't know that, Dani girl," Eddie said, trying to reassure her.

"I'll go inside with you if you want," Bennett offered.

"We need to get back to our residents," she said, suddenly stiffening like she was trying to be brave and professional. "They'll be worried, and we need to decide who's staying with who."

"Okay. We'll come back here later to look in your cottage."

CHAPTER 12

DANIELLE STOOD IN FRONT OF HER HOUSE. IT HADN'T been her home for very long, but she loved it, anyway. She was scared to walk inside and see what had become of her things. Although she wasn't an overly materialistic person, she still valued her personal possessions.

"You ready?" Zach had offered to come with her to check the house out when Bennett, Eddie and Jeremy had gone to help residents pack up and move in with other residents. The whole island was a mess, and everyone was buzzing around with anxiety.

"I guess so." She walked up the walkway and then to the steps. They looked like they were still in good shape, so she stepped up. Zach wasn't far behind,

ready to catch her if she suddenly fell. She appreciated their new friendship right now more than ever.

They walked across what was left of the front porch
and into the house, and her eyes filled with tears. There
were several inches of water across the floors, evidently
trapped when waves battered the house. There was
something to be said for not living on the very tip of an
island. She seemed to get hit harder than anyone else.

"Oh, Danielle…"

"This is awful."

"I can't believe this."

"I need to check my bedroom. That's where I
kept my laptop and all my personal stuff, like old
photo albums."

They walked - or sloshed - down the hallway
toward her bedroom. The sound of water in her
house made her want to break down into a full-
blown crying attack, but she held herself together.

"Where are your photo albums?" Zach asked as
they entered her room. She looked down as a pair of
her favorite sneakers floated by, as if to say "see ya
later, lady" as they headed outside for bigger
adventures.

"In the top of my dresser there," she said,
pointing across the room. For some reason, her feet
felt frozen in place as she tried to take it all in. There
was nothing she could see that was salvageable at

this point. Everything would easily turn moldy as soon as the waters receded.

"Look," he said, turning around and smiling. "I think these are okay." He handed her a thick black photo album. She recognized it as the one that held most of her childhood memories - pictures from Girl Scouts, her first movie ticket stub, pictures from prom. Steeling herself, she took the photo album and opened it.

Relief washed over her as she saw pictures - *dry pictures* - and mementos, protected behind sheets of plastic. Thank goodness she'd put them up high enough to give them a fighting chance. The first thing she was doing when she got back on her feet was getting everything digitized, so she'd never have to worry about losing it again.

"I can't believe these survived." She hugged the first photo album to her chest as Zach retrieved the rest of them. He put them into a plastic container he'd brought and snapped the top on tightly.

"Where would your laptop be?"

"I usually keep it over here beside the bed," she said, turning to look. The laptop was on the floor, down below the inches of water, like a big, expensive paperweight. "Well, I guess I need a new laptop. At least I can use the one at the clinic, since it seems to be in good shape."

"Laptops can be replaced," Zach said, picking up the container. "Ready to get out of here?"

"Let me grab some clothes out of this dresser, and see if I can find any personal items that didn't get destroyed..."

She wandered around the house, basically looking for anything that wasn't wet. She found three shirts, a pair of shorts and a skirt in her dresser. Her other clothes were washable for the most part, so she put them in a plastic garbage bag she found in her laundry room. She'd borrow someone's washer and dryer later.

Then she went to the bathroom and got her hairbrush. Her toothbrush was inexplicably missing, but she could get a new one from the small grocery store on the island.

"I found some food that still looks fine," Zach called from the kitchen. He tossed some canned goods and a few bags of pasta into the container. "Refrigerator lost power, so none of this stuff if salvageable. Plus, I can barely crack the door open because of all the water."

"Anybody home?" Danielle stopped in her tracks when she heard Bennett's voice.

"Back here," she said from the bathroom. Bennett waded over to her.

"Danielle, I'm so sorry about your place. I guess it wasn't as protected as the newer structures."

She shrugged her shoulders. "It is what it is. But I will need a place to stay until we can figure this out."

"They're going to have to build a whole new structure, don't you think?" Zach asked as he walked up. Bennett nodded.

"Yep. This place isn't fixable. I'll call contractors as soon as we get phone service again. But I'm not sure how long it will take."

"How are the residents?"

"Stunned, many of them. Lots of work to do on those cottages. People are doubling up right now. Dorothy is moving in with Morty. His place was untouched, but hers has roof damage, and some of her antiques got destroyed. She's not a happy camper right now."

"I hate to hear that. I lost my laptop, and my house, of course," Danielle said, looking around.

"Where can Danielle stay? I'd be happy to give up my place…"

"Actually, we need a couple of the men to move in with you, Zach. I was thinking about Paul and Dominic. They both have heart issues, and their places are unlivable right now."

"Good luck with Dominic. He's a bit of an old coot," Danielle said, chuckling.

"What about Naomi? Could she stay with her?"

"We're moving Sylvia and Adelaide in with her.

Eddie gave up his cottage for Norman, and he's staying with Jeremy…"

"It's like a game of musical chairs," Danielle said under her breath.

"Danielle, the long and the short of it is you'll need to stay with me until we can figure this out." Bennett blurted it out quickly, like it was eating him up inside.

She looked at him. "Wait, what? I have to live with you? Surely there is someone else?"

"Not really. The cottages are crammed now that so many were damaged. We were already at full capacity. You know that."

"I'm just going to go have a look out back…" Zach said, his voice trailing away as he made a quick exit.

"Why can't I take Zach's place, and he can live with you?"

"Because I can't have you living alone with two men like Paul and Dominic. Plus, their heart issues are complex, and Zach is a doctor."

She crossed her arms. "I've been taking care of them for this long, but now it matters that Zach is a doctor?"

"Okay, so maybe it's more that I'm not comfortable with you living with two men by yourself."

She rolled her eyes. "But one man is okay? As long as it's you?"

"Look, if you're really uncomfortable staying with me, then I'll rent you a short-term place in Seagrove. Still, that will take a few days or maybe more after this storm. And I'll have to send Jeremy to pick you up each morning and take you home each afternoon. You wouldn't be able to have dinner with the residents…"

"Okay, fine! I get it. I just hope this isn't a ploy…"

"Danielle, it's not a ploy. Our island was just knocked around by a hurricane. I don't have time to play games." She could tell he was tired and getting annoyed with her.

"Just so we're clear, I'm only staying until we can find a better arrangement. One of the cottages has to become available as the repairs get done."

"Of course. We'll move you out as soon as it's feasible. And I won't bother you. I'll treat you just like a tenant. In fact, we can live silently, side by side, and…"

"Very funny. Just help me carry this stuff to the golf cart."

Mamie stood on the dock, her laptop in her hand. She held it open to the sky as if God himself was going to send her enough signal to connect to the internet.

"What on Earth are you doing, woman?" She turned to see Morty standing there, his hands on his hips.

"Trying to get a blasted signal. I need to check my email!"

"I don't pretend to know how all of that stuff works, but I'm pretty sure standing on the dock with your computer pointed toward heaven isn't going to get you connected any faster. Everything's down right now, dear. Patience is a virtue, remember?"

She glared at him. "Don't aggravate me, Morty. I'll throw you in this water."

He held up his hands. "What's gotten into you today?"

Mamie sat down on the built-in bench and sighed. "I was anxious all night thinking about my daughter's email, and now we have daylight but no internet. I need to know what she said. I need to know if she will forgive me."

"Why has this become so important to you all of the sudden?" He sat down beside her.

"It's not all of the sudden, but I guess being in a hurricane sort of made me think about life, you know? It's so precious and so short. I've been a big fool, Morty. All these years, I've cared more about what other people thought of me than I did about being a good mom. A good person. I wanted to be revered. I wanted to be envied. I wanted to be that person everyone else wanted to be. And what I turned out to be was alone."

He nodded. "Sometimes we end up alone no matter what we do. I was myself for my whole life, and it ended up not being good enough. At least you can do something about it, Mamie. You can change."

"Well, you should never change, Morty."

He smiled. "I just forgave you a little more."

She looked around. "I can't believe what that storm did to this place. It's going to be a long time before we get back to normal."

"Yeah. I hope they still let people have visitors in a couple of weeks."

"Visitors?"

"The quarterly family visitation is then. I'd hate for everyone to miss their family visits. Of course, it never affects me, but so many people look forward to it."

"I don't think I'll have any visitors either. Maybe you and I can drown our sorrows in a bottle of wine and watch old Dorothy Monroe movies," she said, laughing.

"Dorothy doesn't get visitors either, so I doubt she's going to want to watch her own movies."

Mamie sighed and closed her laptop. "We're just a bunch of old rejects, huh?"

"I suppose so, although I have hope that I'll get to

meet my great niece. I guess there's that. Maybe she can do some energy healing on my sore hip."

Mamie giggled. "She's not a miracle worker, Morty. That hip is old!"

Danielle stood in Bennett's guest room. She felt so uneasy. Not because she was staying with Bennett, but more because she didn't have all her things anymore. She was just standing there in a blank room with a bag of wet clothes, a few photo albums, and a hairbrush. If she was honest with herself, she might've been a bit in shock.

After all, she'd gone from having a healthy, loving relationship and living in her own home to being single and homeless in less than a week. It was a little overwhelming.

"Do you need anything?" Bennett asked, standing in the doorway.

"I honestly don't know," she said, not turning around. Looking at him made her want to hug him, and right now, she needed a little distance from him. That was kind of hard now that she was living in his house.

"The sheets were just washed, and if you need a heavier blanket, I have one in the linen closet over there."

"Thanks."

"Can I take your wet clothes and wash them for you?"

She turned and held out the bag. "They need drying more than washing."

He laughed. "I think we'll still give them a good wash in clean water rather than ocean water."

"Thanks."

"You hungry?"

She paused a moment to notice her stomach. She hadn't allowed herself to feel hungry since morning. It just wasn't on her radar at all. "I think I am."

"I was going to make hamburgers and fries. Would that work?"

She nodded. "Sure."

"Okay. Let me get these clothes started, and then I'll patty up the burgers."

"What can I do?"

"Nothing. You just chill out. You've had an upsetting day." He turned and walked down the hallway. Danielle followed.

"We've all had an upsetting day, Bennett. I don't get special treatment just because my house almost floated away."

He stopped and turned around, smiling. "Fine. You can cut up the onion slices for the burgers."

She rolled her eyes. "You're going to trust me with such an important job?"

"That's not funny."

Realizing she'd made a joke about trust, Danielle instantly felt bad. "I didn't mean it that way. It was my lame attempt at a joke. Sorry."

He continued to the kitchen and pulled an onion out of his vegetable basket. Placing a knife and cutting board on the counter, he turned back to Danielle. "Don't cut off a finger. Our medical care on this island isn't very good."

"Hey!"

He smiled. "See? I can tell jokes too."

Danielle had never slept so hard in her life. She didn't care much for Bennett's guest room mattress. Of course, he'd given her the previous one when she'd moved to the island, but the replacement wasn't nearly as comfy. Still, she'd been exhausted and a night of sleep was just what the doctor ordered.

Dinner between them last night had been pleasant, although they didn't talk a lot. Or at least they didn't talk about personal things. They discussed repairs on the island, medical care of the residents, and the upcoming family visits.

Bennett was determined that they would still have the family visits. The last thing he wanted to do was take that away from everyone after going through such a stressful time. He didn't know how he was going to accommodate extra people on the island, though. That meant the repairs needed to go into overdrive for the next couple of weeks.

Still, she wouldn't have a place to live. Her cottage was beyond repair and would be knocked down and replaced. But trying to get contractors after a hurricane was definitely going to be a gargantuan task.

Bennett had promised that he would try to find her somewhere else on the island to stay as soon as he could. She hoped that once the residents moved back to their cottages, something would become available, although the math didn't really add up.

She got up and started getting dressed for the day. She figured she would go over to the clinic and see if anybody needed help. If they didn't, she would get out into the community and help with repairs as best she could. She was much more skilled at medical tasks than she was at hammering nails, but she would do whatever was needed.

She heard a knock at the door just as she was putting on her shoes. She walked over and opened it to see Bennett standing there, a plate stacked high with blueberry pancakes in his hand.

"Wow. That's a lot of pancakes."

He laughed. "I've often thought that I should have

a large family of children because I don't know how to cook smaller portions for some reason."

"Or perhaps you could cook for a football team. Or an orphanage. Or a troop of soldiers…"

"Very funny. Do you like pancakes or not?"

"Who doesn't like pancakes?"

He handed her the plate and a small bottle of maple syrup. "Enjoy."

He started to walk away. "Hey. Do you want to help me eat some of these?"

"I already ate. I need to get down to the café and start helping with the repairs."

"Oh. I think I'm going to head over to the clinic and just check things out. See if anybody comes by and needs any medical help."

He nodded his head. "Well, have a good day. I guess I'll see you later."

She walked back into her room and watched him through the window as he disappeared down the road. She hated this. The idea of staying with him, but not being in a relationship, was weird and uncomfortable.

Today, the residents that had stayed on the mainland would be brought back, and some of them would have to bunk with roommates for a while. Everything seemed so up in the air in her life and on Wisteria Island, and she didn't like it one bit.

The next few days were a flurry of activity on the island. Wi-Fi still wasn't back up, and even electricity was spotty. The mainland was having the same issues, so Bennett had opted to keep everyone on the island even though some of them wanted to go to the mainland to try to find Internet. It just wasn't safe to have people going all over the place without a stable way to stay in touch.

Bennett watched as Darryl climbed the ladder while Jeremy held it for him. The roof at the cafe was almost fixed, but there was still so much to do. He'd managed to find contractors from further inland who agreed to come to the island to start fixing cottages. Another contractor was drawing up plans for Danielle's new cottage, but it would be months before her place was ready.

A part of him was happy to have her living with him, but he'd also learned how hard it was to have her there. Every part of him wanted to hold her, touch her, hug her. Instead, they sat across from each other like two acquaintances who sometimes shared a laugh together. There was a sadness that lingered in the air like that perfume his grandmother used to wear that made his eyes itch.

"What's the update?" Bennett asked as Eddie walked up.

"Debris removed. All residents are back on the island and in their assigned places. Two contractors working on four cottages right now. Wi-Fi is still down, though."

"What do we need to do on that?"

"I've got some phone calls in, but cell service is spotty right now too."

Bennett sighed. "This must've been what the pioneers felt like."

Eddie laughed at that. "Yeah, I think it might've been a little harder on them."

"I think I'm going to walk over to the clinic and see how it fared."

"Sounds good."

Bennett walked across the street and opened the door. Nobody was waiting in the front, so he walked to the back and didn't see anyone there either. He opened the first exam room and was surprised to find Danielle curled up on the examination table, seemingly sound asleep.

He watched her for a few moments, the soft rising and falling of her chest, the sounds of her breaths exiting her body. She was the epitome of peace at that moment. He had to wonder why she was asleep in the middle of the day.

"Danielle?" he said softly as he touched her shoulder. She didn't move for a moment, but then started to stir. She held the back of her hand over her eyes, shielding them from the fluorescent light above her head.

"Oh, jeez, what time is it?"

"One-thirty."

She sat up quickly and rubbed her eyes. "I have a patient coming at two. I can't believe I slept for so long. I just wanted to lie down for a few minutes. That's why I didn't turn off the light."

"Are you okay?"

She smiled. "I'm fine. I was just really tired."

"Danielle, are you not sleeping well at my house?"

She shrugged her shoulders. "Maybe. It's just hard, Bennett. Things are... tense. I find myself going to bed at night and staring at the ceiling for a couple of hours."

"I understand," he said, sitting down next to her, their legs dangling off the examination table.

"You're not sleeping well either?"

"I spend a lot of the night wondering if you're okay in there, or if you need anything."

Danielle laughed. "I'm not staying in a hotel. You don't have to worry about me."

He sighed. "But, I do. I worry about you because I love you."

"Bennett..."

"Please let me speak, okay?"

She nodded. "Okay."

"I love you, Danielle. It kills me every time I see

you that we aren't talking about this issue between us. You know, I see all of these older people living here with no significant other, no family, no one to hug them. I don't want to grow old that way."

"I get it. I do. But I can't be with someone who stops trusting me so easily…"

"I need to explain something to you, but I can't do it right now. Eddie and the guys need me back at the cafe. Can we have dinner tonight and talk?"

She smiled slightly. "Yes. I'll cook, okay?"

"Sounds great. I'll see you at home later."

CHAPTER 13

MAMIE COULDN'T BELIEVE WHAT SHE'D DONE. Impulsivity was a real problem for her, and this time she really might get herself kicked off the island.

She turned and looked back to make sure no one saw her. So far, it seemed everyone was so distracted that they'd missed the image of a woman in her late sixties speeding away from the island in a small boat. She wasn't running away; she was trying to get to the mainland to find a working computer.

Yes, she knew it was crazy and she should just wait until Wi-Fi was restored on the island, but patience was last on her list of personal attributes. She just had to know what her daughter had said in her email response.

When she finally made it to the mainland, she sighed in relief. Never in her life had she driven a boat herself. Getting across the still choppy waters was something she didn't want to do again. Of course, she'd have to when it came time to get back to the island.

She pulled up to the dock at Seagrove Island and was surprised to see so much damage. The dock itself was in pretty good shape, with just a couple of boards missing, but there were several trees down near The Inn At Seagrove.

"Can I help you?" a very handsome man asked. He was tall and obviously southern from his accent.

"Sorry for interrupting your day. I'm from Wisteria Island." She stepped out of the boat, holding a rope that was attached to it. Knowing she had to tie it up somehow, she'd grabbed the rope on her way out of the boat. The man, sensing her inexperience, smiled and walked closer, taking the rope from her hand.

"Let me do this for you." He quickly tied the boat down using some fancy knot and then turned back to her. "I'm Dawson Lancaster. My wife and I own the inn here."

"Oh, wonderful. I'm Mamie."

He shook her hand. "How are things on the island?"

"Not great. A lot of damage, and we still don't have Wi-Fi. Electricity is spotty too."

"We've got some damage here too, but mostly trees and so forth."

Mamie looked at him, hopefully. "Do you have Wi-Fi?"

Dawson scrunched his nose. "No, sorry."

Her shoulders fell, and she hung her head. "Dang."

"That's why you came here?"

"Honestly, yes. Right before the storm, I sent a very important email to my daughter. I saw that she responded right before the Wi-Fi died. I'm desperate to know what her email said."

Dawson smiled. "I might have good news for you then. My wife co-owns a bookstore over the bridge there. Last time I talked to her an hour ago, they had Wi-Fi again."

Mamie's eyes widened. "Do you think she'd let me check my email, then?"

"I'm sure she would. Come on. I'll drive you over there."

Mamie grinned as she followed him to his truck. She'd never been so thankful in her life.

"Okay, Jeremy, you hold that end and I'll use the nail gun on this end," Bennett called as they stood on the dock. One of the pieces of railing had come loose and finally fallen, so he wanted to get it fixed as soon as possible.

"Hey, did you park the boat on the other dock?" Eddie asked.

"Yeah, I moved it last night," Jeremy said, looking down at the piece of wood he was holding.

Eddie laughed. "Scared me for a minute. I was worried somebody ran away and took the boat!" The men laughed and went back to work.

"Hey, is that a boat coming this way?" Bennett asked, holding his hand over his forehead.

"Looks like it," Eddie said, squinting his eyes. "We expecting anybody?"

"Nope."

They put down the wood and waited for the small boat to arrive. There was a man driving and a woman sitting in the back of the small motorized fishing boat.

"Can we help you?" Bennett asked.

"This lady approached me and asked if I'd give her a ride out here." The woman smiled slightly and then stood up. She reached into her purse and tried to hand him money. He shook his head. "Not necessary."

"Please, take it. I interrupted your fishing."

He shook his head again. "You didn't interrupt nothin'. I was just hiding from my wife, anyhow."

"Do you know someone on the island? Our family visit time isn't until late next week…"

"My mother lives here. I haven't been able to reach her since the storm."

"Our phone and Wi-Fi have been down for a couple of days, but everyone is just fine. Please, let me help you." Bennett reached out and held her hand as she stepped out of the boat.

"I'm glad to hear everyone is okay. My mom emailed me right before the storm, and I responded but never heard back. That wasn't like her, so I guess I was worried."

"Do you live on the mainland?"

She laughed. "No. I live in Maine, actually."

"Maine? Wait. So you flew to South Carolina and then jumped on a fishing boat?"

She nodded. "It sounds kind of crazy when you say it."

Bennett paused for a moment. "Who's your mother?" He thought he knew the answer, but wanted to be sure.

"Mamie Patterson." She looked almost embarrassed to say her mother's name.

"Ah, yes. Mamie."

She smiled. "I hope she hasn't caused any trouble here, but something tells me she has. To be honest, we haven't spoken in a couple of years, but my

brother was worried and asked me to please check
on her after the storm. So, here I am."

"Your brother lives in the Philippines, right?"

"My mother told you?"

"Yes. We've had some conversations."

"I'm sure I sounded like a terrible daughter in
those conversations."

Bennett shook his head. "No, I don't think so."

"Well, since I'm here, would it be possible to see
her?"

"Of course. Hey, Eddie, do you mind taking... I'm
sorry, what's your name?"

"Connie."

"Can you take Connie over to see Mamie?"

"Sure!" Eddie pointed toward the golf cart, and
Connie climbed in.

"Don't give her whiplash," Bennett said in passing
as Eddie walked toward the vehicle.

A few minutes passed before Eddie drove back
up to the dock with Connie still in the golf cart.
Bennett wondered what was going on. Maybe things
didn't go well with her and Mamie, although that
seemed awfully quick.

"Back so fast?" Bennett said as they exited the
golf cart. Eddie looked flustered.

"Mamie wasn't at her cottage or anywhere else
we checked. I'm a little worried..."

"Oh, I'm sure she's just visiting with someone,"

Bennett said, smiling at Connie. Eddie leaned in closer.

"Bennett, the boat's gone."

"What?"

"The boat isn't at the other dock. Someone untied it and took it."

Bennett pulled him closer so Connie couldn't hear them. "You think Mamie went out on the boat alone?"

"I think so. She's been asking a hundred times a day when the Wi-Fi was going to be up. My guess is she headed toward the mainland to see if she could find Wi-Fi."

"And we don't have another boat here. Dear Lord, now what?"

Eddie shrugged his shoulders. "I don't know, boss."

"Do you know where my mother is?" Connie asked, walking closer.

"Not at the moment, but I'm sure she's around here somewhere. She couldn't go far; it's an island for Pete's sake! Let me go check with a couple of her friends. Why don't you have a seat over here at our cafe, and I'll have Agnes make you a nice bowl of soup? She makes a mean clam chowder."

Connie followed him. "Wait, my mom has friends?"

"Take a deep breath in and hold," Danielle said, running her stethoscope over Edna's back. "Your lungs sound a lot better. Did you finish your antibiotic?"

"Yes, I finished it just yesterday," she said, her voice still a bit hoarse. She'd had pneumonia recently, but that seemed much better.

"Keep using your inhaler and doing those daily breathing treatments. We'll get a new x-ray next week, okay?"

"Okay," she said, sliding off the table.

"How'd your cottage fare during the storm?"

She sighed. "Roof damage, darn it. I'm having to bunk with Estelle. She snores like a freight train, and her house smells like mothballs."

Danielle giggled. "Well, count yourself lucky. My house is a total loss and has to be rebuilt."

"Oh, dear!"

"Danielle?" Bennett's voice reverberated through the office, and she could hear an urgency in it.

"Room two!" she called back. He came around the corner quickly and seemed out of breath.

"Oh, hi, Edna. Sorry, I didn't mean to interrupt."

"It's fine. We just finished. I'll see you next week, Edna," she said, waving as Edna walked out of the room and through the waiting area. They waited for the little bell on the door to ding and then Bennett turned his attention back to Danielle.

"We have a big problem."

Danielle walked out of the exam room and back to the center area. She sat on one of the stools to rest her feet. "What's up?"

"Mamie's daughter randomly showed up on the island today."

Danielle's eyes widened. "Seriously? How did she get here?"

"She flagged down a fishing boat, of all things."

"Mamie will be thrilled to see her!"

"That's just it - Mamie is gone."

"Gone? What do you mean?"

"She's not on the island, and the boat was taken. We assume she took off looking for Wi-Fi."

Danielle covered her mouth with her hand. "Oh, no... Does her daughter know?"

"Nope. I don't know how to tell her. We could get sued if something happens to her mother. I never thought anyone would take the boat."

"We need a better system for tying it up, I guess."

He nodded and laughed. "Oh, trust me, that boat will be locked down so Houdini can't get it disconnected from the dock next time."

"So what do we do?"

"I don't..."

"Bennett? You in here?" Eddie called from the waiting room.

"We're back here."

"Everybody decent?"

Danielle laughed. "No, we're all naked back here. Come join us!"

Eddie peeked through the doorway, obviously worried she was being serious. "Oh, hey, ya'll."

"What's going on?" Bennett asked.

"I thought you'd like to know as soon as possible that William from Seagrove just showed up in his boat."

Danielle and Bennett stood up quickly. "Well, he has some pretty great timing," Danielle said as they all ran out the door.

"Are we ever glad to see you!" Danielle said when she saw William on the dock. He was holding two cases of bottled water.

"I thought ya'll might need some extra supplies. I've got more water in the boat, and SuAnn sent along a bunch of muffins and pound cake from her bakery. Is everybody okay here?"

Bennett and Danielle took him aside. "Thank you for the supplies. We are so grateful," Danielle said.

"But we need help. One of our residents stole our boat and went to Seagrove a few hours ago."

"You mean Mamie?"

Danielle put her hand on her chest. "You saw her?"

"Just for a second. Dawson was walking her through town. I think they were heading for the bookstore. Said she needed Wi-Fi. That's when I realized ya'll might need some help over here, so I gathered up some items and headed this way."

"You're a lifesaver," Bennett said, slapping his shoulder.

"So, Mamie was okay?"

"Yeah. Dawson said he'd drive the boat back with her later, and I'll stay here and lend a helping hand until he gets here."

"Thank you so much, William!" Danielle said, hugging him.

"Did I hear someone mention my mother's name? I'm getting a little concerned."

"Connie, this is William, a friend of ours from over in Seagrove."

"Nice to meet you."

"And this is Danielle, our island nurse."

"Nurse? Is my mother okay?" She had a real look of concern in her eyes. And that made Danielle feel better about Mamie's chances of having a relationship with her daughter again.

"She's fine. The truth is, Mamie saw that you sent her an email response to her message, but our Wi-Fi went down and she couldn't open it. It has been all she's talked about for days, and today she untied our only boat and took off to the mainland, apparently looking for Wi-Fi. We had no idea until you arrived looking for her."

Danielle and Bennett waited for her response. "That sounds like something my mother would do," she finally said, rolling her eyes and then chuckling.

"She's a character, for sure," Bennett said, his voice a bit shaky.

"Look, I know she's probably given you some trouble since she's been here, and if she has, I'm so sorry. She has issues with boundaries, obviously. She's also not the most trustworthy person you'll ever meet."

"But she loves you so much," Danielle said, knowing she had no right to stick her nose in their business.

Connie smiled slightly. "I wish love was always enough."

She had a point.

Mamie couldn't remember a time she'd been so nervous. She sat in the little bookstore, which was just adorable, and stared at the blinking cursor on the screen. Julie, one of the owners of the store, had logged her in and told her she could use the computer as long as she needed. She even brought her a muffin and a cup of coffee. Small towns were the best.

Unable to contain herself any longer, Mamie typed in her email password and waited for the screen to load. The Wi-Fi was still a bit slow after the storm, but at least she was going to get connected. When her email popped up, she immediately scrolled down until she found her daughter's response.

Steeling herself for whatever the email might say, she took in a deep breath and blew it slowly out until her lungs were empty. Then, she clicked on the email and started to read.

Mom,

I have to say that I was really surprised to get your email. I had no idea you had moved, so I'm glad to know where you are. Charlie told me he hadn't spoken to you in a few weeks, and he really wished that you would keep him in the loop. Being all the way in the Philippines, he sometimes gets worried about you.

I know you want me to say something about your apology and what is going on between us, but I don't really know what to say. I think about you often, and I miss our relationship. I would be lying if I said otherwise.

But how do I let things go? You're supposed to be able to trust your mother with anything. I don't know how to let you into my world without always fearing that you would betray me again.

Still, I'm more open to talking about this than I was in the past. I've had time to heal some of the wounds. My husband recently lost his mother, and he was very close to her. As I watched him grieve that loss, I thought about how I don't want either of us to leave this earth with bad feelings between us.

Just know that I'm thinking about you and praying for your safety during the storm and always. Give me some time to think, and I will get back to you. I don't know where to go from here, but I hope we can both move forward and build some kind of relationship, even if it isn't what we had before.

Connie

Mamie sat there staring at the email and noticed that the words started to blur. That's when she realized she was crying.

"Oh no, are you okay? Did you get bad news?" Julie asked, handing her a tissue. Mamie hadn't told her why she needed to check her email.

She smiled. "No, not bad news. Just emotional news. Thank you so much for letting me use your computer."

"Are you going to be okay?"

"Yes. I am definitely going to be okay."

"Dawson will be back shortly so he can get you back over to the island before it gets dark. Feel free to take as much time as you need on the computer or grab a book to read."

She smiled gratefully. "Thank you so much for your hospitality. I really will have to come over to the mainland more often. You have an adorable place here. Can I ask you for one more favor?"

Julie nodded. "Of course."

"Would it be okay if I printed out this email?"

"Absolutely," Julie said, walking over to turn on the printer.

CHAPTER 14

CONNIE SAT NERVOUSLY AT THE TABLE. WHEN THEY told her to wait in the cafeteria full of other residents, she didn't realize how boisterous the place would be. These were not typical older people. Everybody was laughing, joking, and smiling.

She remembered when her grandmother had been placed in an assisted living center and how dark and sad the place always seemed to her. It had been a nice place, an expensive one. But it still seemed sad. She eventually realized that the feeling she felt in that place was one of hopes lost. People with no hope exude sadness.

Wisteria Island was nothing like that. These people still had plenty of life left in them. They were excited, social and lively. She'd had a chance to talk to Danielle and Bennett throughout the day while she waited for her mother to come back to the island. They told her how everything was structured, and she felt a sense of relief that her mother was living there now.

Though they'd had a checkered history in recent years, she wanted only the very best for her mom. After all, even though she'd always been a little bit difficult to deal with, her mother had taken good care of her and her brother Charlie. She had been a hard worker and a loving mother for so many years.

Knowing that her mom would have hobbies and friends and great medical care just made Connie feel so much more comfortable. Even if they couldn't repair their relationship, at least her mom would be taken care of by people who only wanted the best for her.

"They should be here soon. Julie, Dawson's wife, was able to give us a call when they left the island. I'm sure it will only be a few more minutes. Your mother is going to be so surprised to see you sitting here," Danielle said as she stood next to her.

"Everybody seems so happy here."

Danielle smiled. "We work hard to make sure they're happy. Some of them are problem children, I have to admit. But they are all quirky and fun in their own unique ways."

As if on cue, a short man came walking up to the table and twirled around in a circle in front of

Danielle. He was wearing a baby blue jumpsuit with bedazzled shoulders and a pair of white cowboy boots. Atop his head was a white cowboy hat with a big purple feather sticking out of the side. Connie didn't know if there was some kind of costume party or what.

"I'm so glad that none of my wardrobe got damaged in the storm!" he said to Danielle, twirling around one more time, the click of his cowboy boots making a noise against the wooden floor.

"Connie, I'd like to introduce you to Morty. He's definitely our most eccentric resident on Wisteria Island."

Morty bowed and stuck out his hand like he was meeting the queen. "Nice to meet you, Connie. You look far too young and pretty to be on this island, so can I assume you're related to somebody here?"

"Yes, my mother lives here, but it appears she has stolen the boat and taken herself to the mainland in search of Wi-Fi."

Morty stopped smiling, put his index finger against his lips and made a hmm sound. "Let me guess who that might be. Mamie?"

"How did you know that?"

"She's been in search of Wi-Fi for a couple of days because her daughter… Wait. You're the daughter? The one who hasn't spoken to her in a couple of years?" He sat down beside her like he was ready for the world's juiciest gossip session.

"Morty! That's none of your business!" Danielle said, slapping him on the shoulder.

Connie held up her hand. "No, it's fine. I see my reputation precedes me. And did my mother explain why we haven't spoken?"

Morty nodded his head and reached over, squeezing her hand. "Yes, your mother told us. She took full responsibility for what she did, but she has pulled a shenanigan here as well. That's why she's going to therapy."

"Morty!" Danielle said again. "I'm sorry, Connie. This is really none of our business, and we're going to go away now. Come on, Morty," she said, pulling on his arm.

Connie really wanted to hear more of what he had to say, but Danielle took him away so quickly she didn't get a chance. But it was good timing because when she turned around in her chair, she saw her mother walking through the door.

Mamie didn't see her. She was busy speaking with some of the other residents and walking toward the food line. Connie waited until she got her tray, and then she saw Danielle walk up to Mamie and point her finger in Connie's direction.

Mamie's eyes were as wide as saucers when she spotted her daughter. She didn't exactly smile, but her face drained of any color as she slowly made her way to the table where Connie was sitting.

She set her tray on the table and stared at her daughter like she was seeing a ghost. "Connie?"

"Hi, Mom."

Mamie slowly sat down across from her and pushed her tray aside. "I don't understand. I just read your email. In fact, I printed it out." She pulled a folded piece of paper out of her pocket and held it up.

"I couldn't reach you after the storm. When I didn't hear back from you on email, Charlie got worried."

"Oh. Charlie asked you to come here?"

Connie sighed. "All right, maybe I was a little worried, too."

Mamie smiled. "You were worried about me?"

"You're still my mother. I don't want anything bad to happen to you."

"Oh, Connie, I'm so sorry for what I did. I'm determined to change. Please don't give up on this old broad."

"Mom, I don't know where to go from here. I don't know exactly what to do."

Mamie reached across the table and took her hands. "I made a couple of mistakes here also, and Bennett was kind enough to offer me therapy. He said I could stay on the island as long as I got some help for my trust issues. I start therapy in a few days. It's on the computer. Maybe if you could stay through the family visit, we could see my therapist together?"

Connie was surprised. Her mother had always made fun of people who went to therapy. "The family visit?"

"Yeah, a few times a year they allow family to come visit and stay for a week. I think the families are arriving next week, so if you could stay a few days, then maybe we could spend some time together too?"

There was no reason Connie couldn't stay. Her husband was back at home taking care of their baby, and he expected that she would be gone for at least a few days. Plus, they had a nanny, which was one of the perks of marrying a man who was successful in his business.

"Okay."

"Okay?"

"I'll stay. And I'll go to therapy with you. And then we'll see where we are."

Mamie squeezed her hands again. "Thank you. I promise I won't let you down this time."

Danielle pulled the chicken out of the oven and set it on a hot pad on the counter. She loved making parmesan chicken, but she especially enjoyed it when she had some great garlic bread to go with it. Thankfully, she found some in Bennett's freezer.

He'd been working with the guys all day on repairs, so she expected him home at any moment. Unsure of how this dinner was going to go, she was trying to prepare herself for either a final breakup or a makeup. She didn't know how she was going to feel once they talked.

She popped the garlic bread into the oven and then finished cutting up the onions for the salad. She made her favorite Italian vinaigrette to go on it, although she was pretty sure that Bennett was going to grab the ranch dressing out of the refrigerator no matter what she did. He had an obsession with ranch dressing.

As if on cue, she heard him turn the key in the front door. When he walked in, he headed straight to the kitchen, following the smell.

"What is that glorious aroma?"

"Parmesan chicken, and I just put the garlic bread in the oven."

"That's why I love you. You can make the best Italian food I've ever seen from a non-Italian person," he said, hanging his keys on the hook by the laundry room door.

He loved her. He was still saying that, even though she said that she wanted a break. She wasn't sure if that was him trying to pressure her or he was just stating a fact.

"Everything should be ready in just a few minutes. I'm sure you want to take a quick shower or change clothes?"

He smiled. "Is that your way of telling me I stink?"

She scrunched her nose. "I didn't want to say anything..."

"Fine. I'll go take a quick shower while you finish getting everything ready. There should be a nice bottle of red wine over there on the counter."

He said it with such ease, like everything was perfectly fine. Maybe he was thinking of this as a date, but she wasn't. She was thinking of it as a conversation, a resolution to whatever was going on.

If there was one thing that Danielle hated, it was unfinished business. While she didn't like conflict, she preferred to get things over with as quickly as possible. She didn't like to linger in the negative feelings.

This "break" that she had instituted didn't feel good anymore. In fact, the moment she blurted it out of her mouth that night, she'd regretted it.

She finished working on everything in the kitchen and set the table just as Bennett was coming out of the back of the house. His shower was quick, but then wasn't that the way with most men?

"What can I help you do?"

"Not a thing. Just have a seat."

She opened the bottle of wine and poured a little into each glass. It hadn't been her intention to make this seem like a romantic dinner, but wine certainly made it feel that way.

They each made their plates and started eating, and she could tell that Bennett was starving. She wondered if he had even stopped for lunch during the day. Everything that had gone on with Mamie and her daughter, plus all the repairs he was working on, had to be exhausting. She wondered if he really wanted to eat dinner, or if he wanted to go to bed and get some sleep.

She was aware that she was probably over-thinking all of it.

Bennett took a bite of the chicken and moaned. "Oh, my gosh. This is amazing! Thanks so much for cooking. I just couldn't face going to the cafeteria tonight."

She put her napkin on her lap and cut her chicken into bite-size pieces. "I went. I didn't eat, but I did get a chance to sit there and watch Connie and Mamie reconnect. It was a beautiful moment."

"I'm so happy for them. I hope it helps Mamie."

"I think she's really learned her lesson, and I know counseling will help her."

"Thank you for agreeing to have dinner with me tonight."

"We have dinner together all the time, Bennett."

He stopped eating and looked at her. "But this feels different."

"Is it?"

"I hope so. Listen, I wanted to explain something to you. And I don't want you to think of it as an excuse because that's not how I mean it. I just need you to understand something that I've never really talked about before."

"Okay," she said, putting her fork down. There was just something about eating and listening to an emotional story that didn't go together.

"Do you remember when I talked about my one serious relationship I had with a woman named Anna?"

"Yes. You said it was like five years ago? Almost got engaged?"

"Right. We dated for a long time. About 3 years. And I thought she would be the one that I married. Almost every other woman I had dated was mainly interested in me for my money, but Anna never really seemed that way."

This conversation was making her a little uncomfortable because the thought of Bennett ever almost marrying somebody else didn't sit well with her. And the fact that she felt that way also didn't sit well with her.

"So what happened?"

"Well, I went on a business trip to Los Angeles. I had a big deal I was signing, and she had to stay at home because she was working. I ended up signing the deal early, which meant I took an earlier flight home. Anna was always worried when I flew, so she would watch the air traffic app to make sure my flight was still in the air and not crash landing somewhere."

"I can understand that. I'm not a big fan of flying myself."

"A lot of times I would fly private, but this particular time I was going to be taking a commercial flight. Anyway, I wanted to surprise her."

"Why do I feel like I can see where this is going?"

"Because you probably can. It was late at night, and I wanted to surprise her at her apartment. I would usually go there when I got back, but the flight I took was pretty late. So it was about eleven o'clock when I arrived. My Uber dropped me off out front, and I walked up the steps. I noticed there were hardly any lights on, so I thought maybe she went to bed early. I was wrong."

"What happened?"

"I had a key to her place, so I stuck it in the lock

and opened the door. I was afraid I'd wake her up, so I tiptoed up the steps. Her bedroom was upstairs. The door was closed, but I could see light underneath it. It wasn't her overhead light, but I figured it was one of her lamps. When I opened the door, all I saw was a bunch of candles lit everywhere. There must've been twenty of them all over the dressers and nightstands. But I didn't see her anywhere."

"And then what happened?"

"I heard water, so I realized she was taking a bath. I didn't want to scare her and make her think somebody was breaking in, so I called her name, but then I heard a lot of commotion and got worried. I pushed open the bathroom door, and there were even more candles everywhere. That's when I realized she wasn't alone."

"Oh no. I figured that's where the story was going."

"She started screaming. Some guy was running around the bathroom trying to find a towel. I flipped on the light and saw way more than I ever wanted to see of another human being."

"Did you know him?"

Bennett laughed. "Oh yes. It was my business partner who had sent me on the trip to begin with. Originally he was supposed to go sign the deal, but he told me he wasn't feeling well and asked if I could take his place."

"That's terrible!"

"Some punches were thrown, I'm embarrassed to say, and he ran out the front door and down the street. I guess he had to call an Uber. Then I was just left with Anna, who kept saying she never meant for this to happen and she was so sorry. But she never said she wanted to work things out with me. She told me she was in love with him. She said she didn't know how to tell me that before, but they were planning to sit me down when I got back from the trip."

"I'm really sorry that happened to you, Bennett."

"Needless to say, that was the end of the relationship. They got married, then divorced. But the moral of the story is that I quickly learned that I couldn't trust people. I couldn't trust my best friend and business partner of several years. I couldn't trust my girlfriend and possible future wife."

"I understand why you wouldn't trust them."

"And until the night that I saw you and Zach dancing, I trusted you. It made me very scared, but I trusted you. But in that moment, when I saw the two of you, I felt like everything was happening all over again. The only problem is, I love you more than I've ever loved anyone, including Anna. So the devastation just shut me down."

"Why didn't you tell me? Why am I just now hearing this story?"

"It was embarrassing. It was something I didn't

ever want to tell anyone because I feel like I looked like a fool in that situation. But now you know."

"I don't think you're a fool, Bennett. I think you're a guy who trusted people, and they took advantage of that."

"Maybe so, but I didn't realize how much it affected me until I saw you dancing with him. I just flashed back to that time in my life, and I put up a wall around me. That's why I acted so immaturely, and I'm sorry for that."

"Bennett, I've been cheated on. I know exactly what that's like. Of course, mine was a very public humiliation, and I ran from it. You know that's how I ended up here, right?"

"I know."

"You can tell me anything. I understand what that was like for you, and I certainly understand wanting to get away from the situation. Look, we've both been hurt by other people before, and we have some scars from that, but if this is going to work, we have to be honest."

"I agree. I promise I will be straight with you from now on."

"You have to trust me unless I give you a reason not to, Bennett. I have to do the same for you. I can't punish you for Richard's crimes."

He nodded his head. "And I can't punish you for Anna's."

Danielle smiled and reached her hand across the table, taking his. "So we're good?"

"Are we?"

"Yes, we are. I don't want to lose you. I don't want to lose this relationship we've built."

"Neither do I. This has been awful, this break."

"I know. It has for me too, but I'm glad you finally told me the truth. And again, Zach is just my co-worker and friend, okay?"

"I know, I know. But he is handsome…"

Danielle rolled her eyes and then stood up. She sat on his lap, her legs dangling to the side. "There is no other man as handsome as you, Bennett Alexander."

"Well, now, I think that's just the wine talking."

CHAPTER 15

THE DAYS PASSED QUICKLY AS REPAIRS TO WISTERIA
Island took shape. By the next weekend, most of the
cottages had been repaired, debris had been picked
up and everything was running smoothly again.
Danielle could hardly believe the way the island had
been transformed, like nothing had ever happened.
Well, except for the fact that her house was gone.

Bennett had hired a crew from two states over,
who were unaffected by hurricane calls, to come
demolish the home and take away the debris. They
had to use a special boat, but they got it done and
now a blank lot was all that was left of Danielle's
home.

The plan was to start construction of her new
house in a couple of months, but for now she'd
continue staying with Bennett. That was fine with

her because it was nice to come home from a long day to a hot meal with the love of her life. Things had gotten better since their talk, and she was hopeful about their future.

"This knee has been hurting something fierce," Morty said, his legs dangling over the side of the table. She palpated around his knee.

"Right here?"

He winced a bit. "Yes! Ouch!"

Danielle smiled up at him. "Morty, do you think it's because you insist on wearing those heeled boots?"

His mouth dropped open like he was shocked by her words. "Absolutely not! Don't you ever say a thing like that again!" He laughed as he said it, realizing she was probably right but refusing to admit it.

Just as Danielle was about to respond, Morty's phone buzzed in his pocket. "Do you need to get that?"

He pulled it from his pocket and looked at it. "Well, since this thing never rings, I should probably answer it… Hello?"

"Is this Morty?" Danielle could hear the woman say. She pointed for him to put it on speaker, which he did.

"Yes, this is. Who's this?"

"You might not remember me, but I guess I'm technically your niece."

"Darla?"

"Oh, so you do remember me."

"Of course I do. How are you, honey?"

She snorted. "Please. This isn't a social call. I'm calling to ask you to stop talking to my daughter. She's impressionable!"

"Excuse me?" He put his hand on his chest and looked at Danielle with surprise on his face.

Danielle couldn't believe what she was hearing. She would never understand how anybody could treat Morty that way. A part of her wanted to interject her thoughts, but she knew it wasn't appropriate. Morty was a grown man and completely able to handle his own affairs.

"I know you're talking to my daughter, and she's just eighteen years old. She hasn't a clue about anything in the world. I know you've got it in her head that she can run off and do all of this New Age stuff instead of going to college!"

"Listen, I don't know what you're trying to accuse me of, but Lacey contacted me. I didn't encourage her to do anything."

"So you didn't tell her she should do what she wants to do and not let anyone else tell her what to do?"

"Well, not in exactly those words. I told her it was okay to be weird."

Darla groaned. "See? This is why my mother

didn't want to have anything to do with you. I don't know why you encourage weirdness. It makes it so much harder for somebody to get along in the world. I mean, look at you. You're living on some island without any family around because you can't act normal!"

Again, Morty's mouth dropped open. He didn't seem to be angry, but more amused by her words. "Darlin', I'm happy as a clam living on this island with my friends. These people accept me and love me for who I am. That's something I never got from my family."

"Well, I can only assume it's an island full of fellow weirdos then. And I don't want my daughter having anything to do with it. You stop talking to her, or else…"

Morty stood up and put his hand on one hip, the other one jutting out. "Or else what? If I understand correctly, your daughter is eighteen, which means she is an adult. You need to cut the apron strings, honey. You can't do a darn thing. She's able to make her own choices, and that means she's finally free of the criticism of that family."

Danielle had never heard him talk like that before. She wanted to jump up and down and clap her hands and yell woo hoo, but again, probably inappropriate.

"Well, I never!"

"Not surprising."

"What is that supposed to mean?"

"Never mind. You wouldn't get it. Is there anything else you need with me? I have things to do."

"Stay away from my daughter. That's it." There was a click and then she was gone.

Morty laid the phone down on the table and looked at Danielle. "Well, I guess you got a really good peek into my family life. That's pretty much how it went from the moment I became a teenager."

Danielle shook her head slowly. "Morty, I'm so sorry. What is wrong with them? You're an amazing person. You're everybody's favorite!"

"Some families aren't as accepting as you. I was always the black sheep, even when I was a kid. They thought I was weird, I was too much, too flamboyant. Back in those days, people didn't understand people like me. It seems like not much has changed in my family."

Danielle put her hands on his shoulders. "Except Lacey. She is the new beginning for your family."

"I fear she's going to be swallowed up by them. I sure was."

~

Mamie wiped a tear away from her eye as she clicked end on the website page. She looked at her daughter, who was also dabbing at her own eyes.

"Wow."

"Yes, wow," Connie said. "That was quite a session. This counselor is very good."

Mamie nodded and then stood up to pour herself another cup of coffee. "Yes, she's amazing. I never thought I would love a counselor so much. Want another cup?"

"No, thanks. I'm so happy that you agreed to counseling, Mom. I can already see you changing."

"I can feel it. Of course, I didn't have much choice in the matter when it came to getting counseling. They were going to kick me off the island like one of those reality TV shows."

Connie laughed. It had been so long since they had laughed together. "Well, I'm still glad you're doing it. I needed it too, and not just because of what happened between us. In fact, I might find a coun-selor when I get back home. I have some stuff I want to talk about, just with being a mom and my marriage and all that stuff."

"Good, honey. I think it will serve you well. I certainly plan to do it for a long time to come. I have a lot of bad habits to unwind." She sat back down at the table and took a long sip of her coffee. There was just nothing better than a nice cup of coffee. It was her favorite part of the day.

"So, I hear the families are coming today?"

"Yes. We all go down to the dock and wait, just to be supportive to the other people. At least, that's what Morty told me. Nobody ever comes for him, but he always goes down there and encourages everybody else. There are quite a few residents who don't get any visitors at all, ever."

Connie's eyebrows furrowed together. "Really? That's incredibly sad."

"Well, to be fair, I would've been standing there alone this time, too. If I hadn't sent you that email, there would be nobody here to greet me, either."

Connie put her hand over her heart. "And that thought makes me so sad, too. I can't imagine you standing out there and nobody coming. It's awful."

Mamie reached over and squeezed her daughter's hand. "Well, thankfully, I don't have to worry about that now."

Morty and Dorothy stood near the dock, each of them well aware they'd be watching the happiness of other people as family members stepped off the boat.

"I hate pasting on a fake smile," Dorothy said.

"It's what we rejects have to do, though, isn't it?"

She nodded. "I suppose. I still can't believe that shrew of a woman called you and said those things. If I were younger, I'd have a rumble with her out behind the woodshed."

Morty let out a loud laugh. "Dorothy Monroe, have you ever been in a rumble?"

"Once. When I was in high school."

"Really? You'll have to tell me that story sometime."

She giggled. "Not much of a story. Cecilia Rochester was the worst bully in our school. She kept picking at me, and one day I just punched her square in the mouth in front of about ten other kids. Well, word got around that I was tough, and she never bothered me again. Neither did anybody else. Then I grew about four inches over a summer, and even the boys were scared of me."

He looked up at her. "I can imagine."

"Oh, look, here they come." She pointed off in the distance at the larger boat Bennett had hired to transport the family members.

For the next fifteen minutes, family members walked off the boat one by one, greeted by hugs and smiles. Morty envied his fellow residents. Oh, how he wished he had a supportive family who loved him. Sometimes, he thought he might just trade everything he had for that kind of love.

"Do you want to get some ice cream after this?" Dorothy asked.

"Sure. We can drown our sorrows with butter pecan."

"I think a nice chardonnay might pair well with that," she said, laughing.

They were just turning around to walk back toward town when someone called Morty's name.

"Are you Morty?"

He turned back to see a young woman with long blond hair standing there, a duffel bag in her hand.

"That's me. And you are?"

She smiled broadly. "I'm Lacey."

Morty felt butterflies suddenly take flight in his stomach. He couldn't believe someone had traveled to see him. A family member? At that moment, he felt so important. So loved.

"Lacey?" he said, walking closer. "My goodness, you're so beautiful! Look at that hair!"

She laughed. "I knew exactly who you were when I saw you. My mother described you to me a while back, and I found some old family photos. You're kind of…"

"Short? Yes, darlin', I know."

"I'm so glad to meet you!"

He grinned. "I can't believe someone from my family came all this way to see me. I never thought that would happen."

"I told you I wanted to meet you, so here I am. Do you mind if I give you a hug?"

"I thought you'd never ask!" He pulled her into a tight hug and relished the moment he was finally accepted and loved by someone in his own blood-line. It was miraculous and amazing. "Come on, we'll go to my cottage and get you settled in." They started to walk when Morty noticed Dorothy standing back, looking out at the water. He turned around and pulled on her arm. "Lacey, this is my friend, Dorothy Monroe. She's also like family to me now. Do you mind if she comes with us? We can have some ice cream."

Lacey smiled. "I would love that! Nice to meet you, Dorothy."

Dorothy looked shocked, but then smiled. "It's nice to meet you too, Lacey. I don't want to inter-fere, though, Morty."

He waved his hand at her. "Like I said, this is our time for a family visit, and you're my family, too. Come on."

Morty couldn't remember a time where he was more enthralled in a conversation. Lacey was only eigh-teen years old, and nobody ever said eighteen-year-olds were all that interesting, but this was the first real family he had had in decades, and he was soaking in every word she had to say.

"I was really involved in dance. I took ballet when I was a little girl, and I'll never forget my first recital."

"I always wanted to take ballet, but that wasn't acceptable back in those days," Morty said.

"I bet you would've been great at it. So, anyway, I also went to math camp most summers. My mom liked to have time for herself, especially after my dad left. So, I spent four weeks at math camp even after I didn't want to go anymore."

"Math camp sounds terrible," Dorothy said, scrunching her nose.

"It wasn't so bad. Helped me pass algebra in high school. But I really wasn't into it. Mom said I needed to get good grades to get into college, but I started thinking that maybe I didn't want to do that."

"Not everybody needs to go to college," Morty said. "Differences are what make the world go round."

She smiled. "I've always loved to draw. For a while, I thought about going to art school. I even applied and got accepted, but I never told my mom because she wasn't open to me pursuing art. She's even less open to me pursuing energy work."

"Listen, I'm sure your mother loves you and wants the best for you, but now that you're an adult, you have the right to make choices for your life. After all, nobody else has to live your life but you. If you want to pursue art or energy healing or even ditch digging, it's nobody's business but your own. Of course, that means you have to support yourself financially."

She nodded her head. "I know. I worked all through high school, and I saved every penny because I didn't really have a social life, anyway. Plus, when I applied to art school, I got a scholarship. I've been thinking a lot about it lately."

"When I became an actress, my family was totally against it," Dorothy said, taking a bite of her ice cream. "But it had been my dream since I was a very little girl, and it turned out to be quite a success. Now what would've happened if I had done what my family wanted me to do?"

Morty loved this moment of the wise two older people counseling the young girl. It felt like a scene from a Disney movie or something.

"Where is this art school?" Morty asked.

Lacey smiled. "It's in Savannah. That means I would be just a couple of hours from you."

Now Morty really wanted to encourage her to go to that school, but he didn't want to be like his family. This wasn't his decision. This was Lacey's life, and he was bound and determined to do whatever he could to just support her.

"Oh, wow. Wouldn't that be something?"

"Uncle Morty, would you like for me to be that close to you?"

He reached over and held her hand. "Of course, dear. But I'm not going to pressure you. I know that no matter where you live, we will still be close. We can always do video calls, right?"

There was a part of him that was trying to hold on to her as tightly as he could. What would happen if she left the island, and he never heard from her again? It was that sense of abandonment that was very deep within him, and he figured it would always be there.

"I'm so glad I was able to come."

"Me too. What did your mother have to say about it?"

She plastered on a very fake smile. "She doesn't know where I am."

"Pardon?"

"Well, I sort of packed my things and ran away from home."

"Oh dear," Morty said, well aware that this was not a good thing. "Lacey, as much as you might be mad at your mother, you simply must call her and let her know you're safe. She's got to be worried."

"Tell her I'm on Wisteria Island? She would have a fit!"

"I know. But she'll likely blame me instead of you. And what do I care?"

"Do I have to?"

"Yes, you do. Where is your phone?"

"It's actually dead. Maybe I can just call her later…"

He slid his phone across the table. "You can use mine."

Lacey sighed. She picked up the phone and dialed the number, waiting for her mother to answer.

"Mom? Yes, I know. I didn't mean to worry you.… I'm fine… I'm actually on Wisteria Island… Stop yelling at me! I wanted to visit my uncle… I like him…" She tried to muffle the phone with her hand in an effort not to offend Morty. "I'll be home in a couple of days.… I'm an adult! You can't tell me what to do… Mom! Listen to me… I've made a decision… Are you listening to me? I've made a decision about college. I was accepted into art school in Savannah on a scholarship, and I've decided to go… It most certainly is a real college!"

Morty didn't pay any attention to the rest of the conversation. All he heard was that his great niece was going to be close, and he might have someone who would come visit him on a regular basis. Heck, maybe he would even go into Savannah from time to time and hang out with her and her friends.

She pressed end on the call and looked at her

uncle, smiling. "I guess you heard that I'm going to go to college right around the corner?"

"I did hear that. And I'm so proud of you, Lacey."

"I'm proud of you, uncle Morty."

"You're proud of me? What ever for?"

"Because you gave me the confidence to be who I am just by being you."

Mamie couldn't believe that the family visits were over. Even though her daughter had gotten to stay extra time at the beginning, it still wasn't enough.

They spent so much time together walking on the beach, eating and laughing that the time seemed to fly by. But she knew Connie needed to go back home to her daughter.

Mamie had gotten to video chat with Connie's husband and her new grandbaby a couple of times. She had a chance to apologize for what she had done wrong before, but more importantly, she had gotten to see that brand new baby.

There was just something about a baby that signaled new beginnings, and she was happy to have one with her daughter and granddaughter. But there was never enough time.

"I'm going to miss you," Mamie said, rubbing her thumb across Connie's cheek.

"I can't believe I'm going to say this, but I'm going to miss you too, Mom. I'm so glad we got a chance to do this."

"Me too."

"Are you sure you don't want to come live with us in Maine? We have plenty of room."

Mamie smiled. "I appreciate that, honey, but you have your own life. I do want to come visit, though. I can't wait to spend time with Gabrielle. I want her to know I'm her grandmother."

"Of course. You let me know when, and we will get the guest house ready."

"You'd better get on the boat, or I might just drag you back to my house and lock the door so you can't leave."

Connie laughed and hugged her mother tightly. "You're doing good things. Keep it up."

Mamie watched as she walked toward the boat, and she had to force herself not to cry. The time they had spent together was like a miracle, and she was so thankful for it.

"I'll call you as soon as I get back, and maybe you can even come help me move into my dorm when college starts."

Morty, who was dabbing at his eyes with an

embroidered handkerchief, hugged her tightly."Of course. I would love to come help you move, and I can also help you decorate your dorm room. You don't want it to look drab."

"I saw your decorating skills, and we might have to talk more about that," Lacey said, giggling.

Morty had really enjoyed spending time with his great niece. He had been able to tell her all kinds of old family stories and build new memories. He hated to see her go, but he also knew that she would be close to him soon.

Until Lacey had visited, he didn't realize just how much he was missing that family connection. He also had always kept that stiff upper lip when other people had family members come for a visit. He wanted to support them, but he was incredibly jealous of their good fortune.

As he watched Lacey board the boat, he waved and smiled, confident in the fact that he was probably going to cry himself to sleep tonight.

EPILOGUE

Six Months Later

Danielle stood in front of her new cottage, a blindfold across her eyes. Bennett had made her promise not to drive by or visit the property for the last few months. A couple of times, she'd almost broken her promise, but trust was a big thing between them and she wasn't risking it.

Still, she was curious. They'd looked at some building plans together right after the hurricane, but she'd left most of it up to Bennett. After all, it was his island, and he was footing the bill for everything. She could only be so pushy.

The only things she'd asked for were a garden tub and a bigger kitchen. Aside from that, she wasn't going to be picky. The house sat at the tip of a beautiful island, so complaining about anything wasn't reasonable. It would be her dream home, no matter what he built there.

This time, the house would be jacked up on stilts to help avoid any flooding in the future when storms or hurricanes hit again. He also had special hurricane shutters installed, and the walls were much thicker. She was thankful for all of those precautions because she didn't want her house to ever have to be torn down again.

"When can I take off this blindfold?"

"Right now," he said, pulling the tie on the back of her head as the blindfold dropped to the ground.

When her eyes adjusted to the light, she couldn't believe what she saw. The cottage was at least twice the size of her previous one, and it stood tall. It was a beautiful shade of yellow with white trim and black shutters, and it reminded her of a house on the streets of Charleston. Her eyes welled with tears when she looked at it.

"Oh, Bennett, it's beautiful! I can't believe I get to live here!"

She turned around and hugged him tightly, planting a long kiss on his lips.

"Wait until you see the inside," he said, smiling. "You'll really want to kiss me then."

He took her hand, and they walked up the front steps and stood on the porch. She turned around and looked at her view. She could see practically all the way into the downtown area of Wisteria Island on one side and on the other side was a beautiful view of the ocean.

"I'm going to be having my morning coffee out here regularly."

Bennett unlocked the door and pushed it open, pointing for Danielle to walk inside. She grinned like a Cheshire cat and walked past him into her new home.

She couldn't believe what she was seeing. Beautiful hardwood floors ran throughout, and she had tile in the kitchen. The whole floor plan was wide open, with a huge island and breakfast bar overlooking the living room from the kitchen.

On the back of the house was a beautiful sunroom and a wall of windows overlooking the ocean. Even from the front door, she could tell that she had a giant deck out back.

"I can't believe you did all of this."

Bennett laughed. "I didn't do anything except pay for it. The contractors did an amazing job."

She hugged him again. "You didn't have to build such a big house for me. I was fine getting my little cottage back."

"Is it crazy for me to want to make sure my best nurse and love of my life stays on this island as long as possible?"

She put her arms around his waist and her cheek

against his chest. "I'm not going anywhere, and that has nothing to do with the size of my house."

"Come on, I want you to see your bedroom and bathroom."

They walked down the hallway, and she peeked into the guest room. It was basic, but Bennett had ordered furniture for all the rooms, so it was ready for a guest at any time. Maybe she would finally invite her mother to the island. Maybe.

They walked into the bedroom and Danielle was surprised to see how large it was. It had vaulted ceilings that were covered in the most beautiful wood slats. She had a sitting area that also overlooked the ocean with a big fluffy chair and table.

When she walked into the bathroom, she was astounded at how large it was as well. There was a jetted garden tub, a tiled shower with a clear glass door and a seat, plus the biggest walk-in closet she had seen in a while.

"Everybody is going to be jealous of my house!"

"Let them be jealous. You deserve it."

"Did I see stairs?"

"You did. There's a bonus room up there, along with another bathroom. I figured you could use it as an office or maybe something else one day."

"Something else? Like what?"

"I don't know. A playroom?"

Danielle started laughing. "For all my toys and blocks?"

Bennett shrugged his shoulders. "Why don't we go out on the back deck?" They walked back down the hallway, through the living room and sunroom and onto the oversized deck that ran the whole length of the house.

"Look at that view," Bennett said, swiping his hand from side to side toward the ocean.

Danielle had never seen anything as beautiful as her new home. Back in the city, even an apartment the size of her kitchen would've cost her thousands of dollars a month. She couldn't believe her good fortune that she got to live in this place.

She slid her arm around Bennett's waist and put her head on his shoulder as they stared out at the water. "Thank you so much for doing this for me."

"You're worth it, Danielle. I would've bought you ten houses if that's what you wanted."

She turned and looked at him. "I believe you. You know, six months ago we were in kind of a shaky place, but I'm so glad we were honest with each other."

He squeezed her hands. "I need to be honest with you about something else."

Her stomach churned a little bit. Anytime someone announced they wanted to have an honest conversation, it had never really gone great for her in the past.

"Okay…"

"I didn't build this house just to replace the old one."

"I'm not sure what you mean."

"I had it built bigger because I would like for more than just one person to live here."

"Do you want me to have a roommate?"

He smiled. "I guess you could say that."

"Can I choose Morty? I think he's the only one I could live with."

Bennett started laughing. "No, you don't get to choose."

She dropped his hands and crossed her arms over her chest. "Okay, what in the world are you talking about?"

"I would like to be your roommate."

"But you have your own cottage."

"Danielle, listen to me." He picked up her hands again and looked into her eyes. "I want us to live here together, and one day I'm hoping our kids will live here too."

"What?" It suddenly felt like a flurry of butterflies were having a dance party in her stomach. Was he saying what she thought he was saying?

Without warning, he suddenly lowered down to one knee and reached into his pocket. She felt like she was in a movie and everything was moving in slow motion.

"I cannot imagine living my life with anyone else. You're my perfect other half, my best friend and the only person I want to sit and watch the ocean with at night. You cook great Italian food, watch trashy reality TV with me, and if I need stitches, well, you're my gal. Danielle Wright, will you do me the honor of becoming my wife?"

She froze in place, her hand over her mouth. Unable to form words, she nodded her head quickly and thrust her left hand out in front of him. He smiled, tears welling in his eyes as he slipped the ring on her finger. It was a beautiful princess cut diamond and looked exactly like the ring she kept on her vision board in her phone, although she'd never even shown it to Bennett.

Bennett stood back up and hugged her tightly. "We're getting married!" Danielle yelled as he spun her around. All of the sudden, she heard people clapping and cheering.

When she turned to look, many of the residents were coming out from underneath the deck where they had apparently been hiding during the whole thing. Zach was also there, a huge smile on his face as he mouthed the word "congratulations".

"We're having a wedding!" Morty screeched,

jumping up and down as he threw confetti in the air. Of course, Morty would have confetti.

Danielle couldn't remember a time in her life when she'd been happier. There was nothing about her life she would change. She had the perfect boyfriend, now fiancé. She had the perfect job. And now she had the perfect house.

In the past, she would've thought something bad must be coming because there was so much good in her life, but she honestly felt peaceful. She felt happy. She felt settled.

"I hope you don't mind that I invited them here for the proposal?"

She smiled and put her head on his shoulder as they looked out over the festivities on the beach behind the house. "Of course not. These people are our family."

"I can't wait to get married and start our own family."

"We have lots of adventures ahead of us, Bennett Alexander."

"Yes, we do, my beautiful fiancée."

See all of Rachel's books in order at www. RachelHannaAuthor.com.

Made in the USA
Monee, IL
29 October 2023

45397792R00136